Weatherly Hall

Weatherly Hall

Andy Hunt

Books by Andy Hunt

Science Fiction/Adventure/Horror

1. *Conglommora*
2. *Conglommora Found*
3. *Conglommora Defense* (upcoming)
4. *Weatherly Hall*

Technical Non-fiction

- *The Pragmatic Programmer: From Journeyman to Master*
- *The Pragmatic Programmer: 20th Anniversary Edition*
- *Programming Ruby*
- *Pragmatic Version Control*
- *Pragmatic Unit Testing in Java*
- *Pragmatic Unit Testing in C#*
- *Practices of an Agile Developer*
- *Pragmatic Thinking & Learning: Refactor Your Wetware*
- *Learn to Program with Minecraft Plugins (Bukkit Edition)*
- *Learn to Program with Minecraft (CanaryMod Edition)*

Acknowledgments

Thanks to all the readers of my novels and tech books over all these many years for your kind encouragement and support. I appreciate all of you!

Thanks to my early reviewers, including

Kerry Buckley, Jorge Castro, Charles Engelke, Patrick Helm, Pratik Karki, Zak Koganitsky, Vinod Kumaar R, and Matthias Merdes.

Thanks also to my copyeditor, Tracy Liebchen, who diligently tracked down my errant commas and fat-fingered typos. Any remaining errors are entirely my fault.

And very special thanks to Ellie, Elizabeth and Stuart, for their help keeping me hip and supporting all of my crazy projects. I couldn't do it without you.

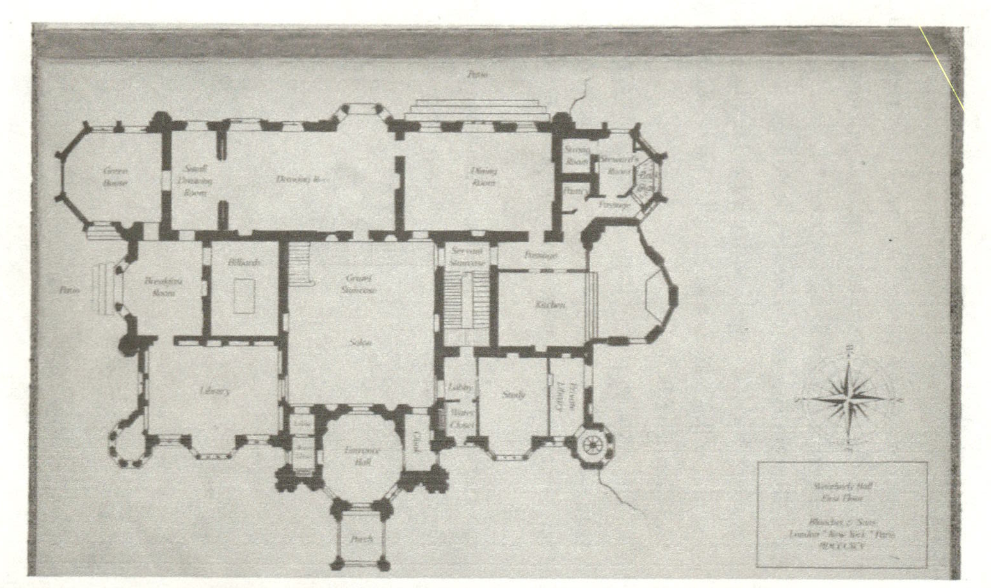

Patio
Green House
Small Drawing Room
Drawing Room
Dining Room
Strong Room
Steward's Room
Pantry
Passage
Breakfast Room
Billiards
Grand Staircase
Servant Staircase
Passage
Kitchen
Solon
Patio
Library
Lobby
Water Closet
Study
Private Library
Cloak
Entrance Hall
Porch
N
Winterbody Hall
First Floor
Blanchet & Sons
London · New York · Paris
MDCCLXX

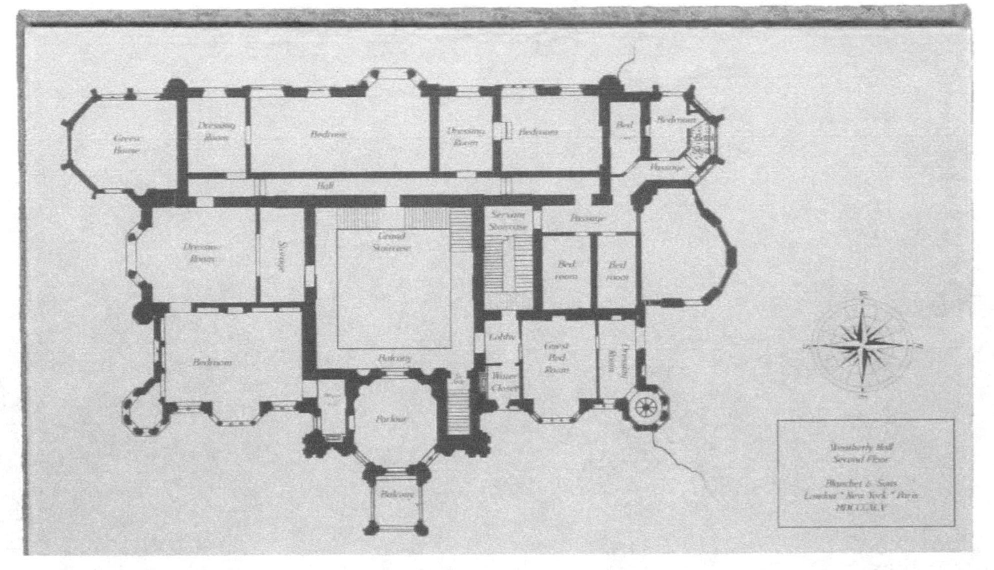

Green House
Dressing Room
Bedroom
Dressing Room
Bedroom
Bed
Bedroom
Passage
Hall
Servant Staircase
Passage
Dressing Room
Storage
Grand Staircase
Bed room
Bed room
Bedroom
Balcony
Lobby
Water Closet
Guest Bed Room
Dressing Room
Parlour
Balcony
N S E W
Wimberly Hall
Second Floor
Blanchet & Sons
London * New York * Paris
MDCCCLV

One

AS-IS. A LONE MANSION atop a steep and isolated hill on the outskirts of a dying former mining town, several hours from the megapolis. Un-renovated, uncomfortable, drafty, hard to heat and cool. This property is offered strictly "AS-IS," no warranty or guarantee expressed or implied.

That's not what the real estate brochure said, but it may as well have. It probably should also have mentioned that the house was built just after the First Civil War, in the late 1800s. Hadn't been renovated much since then— it barely even had electricity, let alone any modern, AI-fueled conveniences.

Which is exactly what Henry wanted. He could be free. Safe. Alone.

He took one last look out the floor-to-ceiling glass windows in his sleek, modern apartment on the seventy-sixth floor. His view of the northern megapolis stretched as far as the eye could see, all the way to the horizon.

He liked the look of glass, of shiny steel. Clean, simple lines. Always light out, always bustling. The megapolis never slept.

Henry had loved all of that at first, but now he was ready for a change. What would it be like to live in a place that was actually dark at night? Actually quiet? He shivered in both excitement and a little fear at the thought of a truly dark night, then turned from the window abruptly—he didn't want to make it *look* like he was staring out the window and thinking.

He'd been very careful while moving out; just a few pieces at a time, so that it didn't look like he was moving out. He would leave all the furniture and most of his "city" clothes. Bank accounts, delivery services, local presence—he'd carefully left them alone, put them on vacation mode, or shut them down over time. Nothing all at once, no sudden moves, and nothing that would trigger any known behavioral patterns of someone about to go off the grid.

La la whee, do whee. His phone chimed a poor rendition of a popular tune—poor not because of lack of a quality speaker but perhaps lack of proper licensing. It wasn't quite the same as the song it was supposed to be. But it got his attention.

He held it up and looked at the message. Someone from work.

Oh, leave me alone already. Assholes.

He started to put the phone back in his pocket, then changed his mind and headed into the galley kitchen instead. It was a narrow, small affair, but he didn't mind as he rarely cooked anymore. Seemed there was never time, and fresh, unprocessed vegetables were just hard enough to get that he didn't bother. He stuck his phone down the sink drain, into the disposal, turned on the water, and switched the disposal on.

A loud, piercing shriek. The cry of tortured and dying metal as his phone was shredded by the mechanism, which did a decent job of inflicting counter-damage to the disposal blades. Sparks flew as the battery exploded with a sharp snap, and a small fountain of glass blew up from the drain like a mini-tornado. He shut the ruined disposal off.

Just leave me alone.

Funny, that used to be the mantra he'd chant when dealing with his dad. Now he felt that with nearly everyone, everything.

It was time to go, now, just in case the missing phone signal raised some kind of alarm for being unresponsive. He poured a cup of coffeesynth into a travel mug, walked out of the kitchen, picked up his coat, and took one long, last look at the view.

Henry stepped out the front door and placed his palm on the luminescent panel. A white glow ran from the top of the panel to the bottom, quickly, confirming his identity from the biomarkers—and not just the ones from his palm. He knew he was also being scanned for facial recognition, posture, and who-knows-what-else. The palm reader was only one small part of the larger sensory net.

He walked down the hall a bit, then stepped into the glass elevator and clenched his stomach against the sudden drop as the car flung itself down dozens of stories. There were a couple of other people in the elevator already; they exchanged curt nods and kept their distance, as was customary in the city, but didn't speak. The elevator was monitored, certainly for voice and video, at least. Identity recognition based on facial scans, or gait analysis, or something, was very likely. Henry couldn't wait to get out of the city, away from the unsleeping eyes always on him. Always on everyone. It was nearly impossible to escape.

Nearly.

But not completely. It was very hard to find any property without sensors, cameras, AI house assistant, or persistent, low-latency comms these days. Most older properties that hadn't been upgraded were just bulldozed and replaced with high-density, cheaper, fully-connected housing, and of course, all public streets and areas within the megapolises were fully monitored.

In fact, this mansion would have been on the National Historic Buildings registry, once upon a time, when there was just one nation and people cared about such things. But they did away with that after the war and bulldozed many of those historic places as well, to make room.

But not this one.

Weatherly Hall had some two-dozen bedrooms, a few baths, a couple of large ballrooms and drawing rooms, and a staircase large enough you could probably hold a wedding on it. Four or five stories—the stats varied depending on the source Henry had read—and an extensive basement. Some of the older portions of the house and outbuildings still had gas lighting, not even electric. And no network connections at all. No voice assistants, no streaming media, no optimized environmental control.

And no surveillance, either. Smack in the middle of nowhere—maybe the edge of nowhere, even—off the grid and overlooked. Henry's own, private, massive, overlooked mansion.

Henry got off the elevator at street level, just as he always would, and made sure the camera in the elevator and hallway saw him. But around a corner, in a camera dead spot, he slipped into a stairway and down to the lowest parking level. It wasn't *supposed* to be a camera dead spot, but he'd paid some local hooligans to smash a few key cameras and sensors. It would look like just random vandalism—he'd been careful to make sure they smashed other, unrelated sensors as well, not just the ones he needed. But now he had a clear shot down to the parking garage, and he calmly, directly, headed to the manual car and trailer he'd bought.

He palmed the sensor, opened the driver's side door, and climbed in. Henry had never driven outside the borders of the megapolis before and wasn't entirely sure what to expect. He patted the sunglasses in his pocket. Would he need those on the open road?

You had to wear them on the trains and hyperloop cars and any other public transportation because of the

UV light. Just one of many anti-viral measures that started after the waves of pandemics swept through. But that was nearly before his time, maybe even before the war.

The car hummed to life, glowing with the soft assurance of old-fashioned reliability. There was no transponder on the car itself, and the cameras at the street exit had suffered the same fate as the ones in the building.

Damn vandals. Henry smiled. He merged into the neat, orderly lines of self-driving cars, just an insignificant speck in the endless flow of traffic now. As he got farther from the central district of the megapolis, he thought he could make up some time and zip in and out between them—but not too aggressively.

There might even be intersections out there. Here in the city, there weren't any as the roadbeds, tubes, and other transport systems all crossed at different levels.

Smooth and even, he reminded himself, resisting the urge to pass a handful of dutifully consistent cars.

Just like an automatic.

For the next few hours, he would be part of the background noise of life in the megapolis. Just a mote in the sea of traffic, going about his business like everyone else. He'd be on the monitors for a long while, and then he'd just be gone, past the outskirts of the megapolis. No one would know where he was.

They'd have no idea he was slowly, painstakingly making his way along backroads, through tiny towns long bypassed by the self-driving car tubes. Traversing the Wastelands, long abandoned, in his human-driven car.

Manual cars weren't entirely unheard of, not yet, but were increasingly rare. The last few that did not yield to the convenience—or maybe the servitude—of the globally connected AI systems still hung on to their vintage manual cars with pride.

It wasn't illegal or anything. But it certainly was viewed as odd, like wearing a heavy winter trench coat in the pavement-melting heat of summer. Sure, you could do it. But you'd get stared at. Judged. Maybe even questioned by the police.

The road stretched out and yawned ahead of him, and Henry almost did the same. He flipped on the satellite feed for some music to help keep him awake. As usual, he was disappointed. What counted as "music" was so sped up, so choppy, it barely registered before a hard cut to some jarring, completely different tone and feel.

Like listening to a high-speed factory robot. Or something. He tried a few different options, skipped past some talking heads bloviating on the state "news" channel.

Well, the "state" part is accurate, at least.

Then he gave up and tried to focus on the scenery instead. Henry watched the sun setting off his left side. Violent, dark orange colors stabbed the sky, with thick black clouds overhead. Long shadows grew over the cracked pavement and through the crumbling buildings.

Didn't need those sunglasses after all.

Even though they called areas like this "Wastelands," Henry thought that was a little melodramatic. These weren't nuclear dead zones—the true wastelands—although there were a few of those on the planet already. Those weren't even named, they were just… dead. Not even drug dealers worked there.

If you want your dodecs or even just diaphane, you won't find it there.

Not to mention more basic needs of food or uncontaminated water. No, these Wastelands were heavily damaged in the war and just not rebuilt. Not enough jobs in the area, no services, not enough reason to stay. So they crumbled into disrepair as people moved into the increasingly dense megapolis-style city networks and abandoned these areas. Henry thought they probably should have just called them "Abandonlands" or something. But Wastelands was close enough. It was a waste, to be sure.

Lightning cracked the sky open, vicious, high-energy bolts. A sudden wind gusted, and he struggled to keep the car on the road. Before he knew it, a blinding deluge dumped more water on his route than he had ever seen. He pulled over, where he *thought* the side of the road should be, and waited for it to pass.

He'd heard of these intense, dangerous storms in the Wastelands. In the megapolis, drones and high-powered lasers nudged the weather patterns to maintain a favorable local environment. Just enough rain when needed, not too much or too little, just enough of a nudge to steer severe storms away and out into the Wastelands.

You couldn't really *control* weather, that was a popular misconception. But you could tilt the balance in your favor to protect the megapolis. But nature being nature, favoring one area likely meant devastating another.

Always a balance. That was something else his father never appreciated. *Dad demanded control, not balance.* He frowned at the memories.

A few more truly alarming lightning displays and the torrential downpour stopped as quickly as it had started. Standing water now covered the flooded roadway; he'd have to be careful. Slowly he eased the car and trailer back on the roadway and continued on.

Just up the road, he passed the half-collapsed remains of what was once a large apartment building. *I suppose you could try and live here. But that's too much wilderness for me.* He shook his head.

The Wastelands were a harsh environment. He wanted peace, quiet, and privacy—but not a fight for survival every day.

Henry had started looking for a new place a while ago: a home, somewhere, that time had overlooked. A place others would reject as inconvenient, but he would embrace for its solitude. And protection. He couldn't be discovered, not now.

They must not find me, he repeated to himself. It had become his new mantra.

He didn't want to apply for the nav data for this trip. That would have been a huge red flag to anyone looking. The automatic cars would only take you to your personally approved locations, and stand-alone map or nav data was hard to come by. Partly that was to control the sporadic pandemics that swept the globe and also just so the state could better keep track of you. But, Henry grinned to himself, he had ways. He got the data he needed—and he had found the house in the first place.

Searching anonymously through national real estate listings, he found Weatherly Hall located in the far north of The Democratic Republic of New Yorkland. He was lucky and wouldn't have to cross the border into Foundry or down south into the New Confederacy. The property was still located within the boundaries of his own country, the country where he was born and raised.

Weatherly Hall was stupidly huge—you could have run it as a hotel easily, or a boarding school, or something like that. But apparently that had never happened. From what Henry had read online, it was only and ever maintained as a private home, at least according to the tax records. And it was *old*. Must be solid to have survived this long; that was his reasoning. Two official world wars, two civil wars, countless foreign incursions, and unceasing global map-redrawing. He shook his head. It never ended, never would end. The latest near-war with Eurasia proved that. But that was the present; Henry preferred to let his mind dwell in the past.

He smiled at that, as the last of the sun gave up and sank into the inescapable darkness. He had to admit a certain nostalgia for anything from before the Second Civil War. Henry had been in his teens then but remembered— or thought he remembered—what the world used to be like. The world his parents knew, and their parents before them.

Nostalgia or not, Henry felt strongly that this was where he needed to be now. Away. Out of the spotlight, out of any lights at all. In the dark, on the edge of the bright lights of pervasive global awareness.

So here he was literally in the dark now, maneuvering his manually-driven car and trailer along pitch-black roads past the Wastelands. There were no other cars, not often, at least. No streetlights, no local guide beacons, no satellite guidance, and no shortage of potholes and broken, crumbling pavement. He sped along in peace.

Perfect.

The hours withered and dropped away as night grew long. Henry caught himself nodding off a few times. In a normal car that wouldn't be a problem, but this was off the grid and off automatic. It was all on him, and he could quite easily crash into the row of dark, solid trees or unforgiving rubble spilled into the roadway. He opened the windows. The air was uncomfortably cold, but it helped keep him awake. A few more hours to go, still.

Suddenly, something large and unnaturally white flashed right in front of his headlights.

He slammed on the brakes and shot a glance in the rear view, where he saw the trailer starting to jackknife, in sickening slow motion. Car and trailer both shuddered as it all skidded sideways off the pavement into the shoulder with a groaning noise, punctuated with the sharp ping of gravel spraying up and ripping into the car. He came to a stop in the ditch as the deer shot past and off into the black.

Shit, fuck, shit shit shit!

Panting, heart pounding, adrenalin racing, Henry had to pause and take a few deep breaths. It would be okay. He'd been so lucky so far, and was *so* close now. But, *shit!*

His right leg was soaking wet from the coffeesynth. The mug had flown right out of the cup holder when he hit the brakes. And that wasn't all—two boxes had slammed into the dash from the passenger seat. He grimaced as he took in the damage, desperately hoping the trailer was still upright and hadn't turned turtle. If it had tipped, he'd need a tow truck, or official help. And that was attention he could not afford. Not now.

He got out of the car and walked behind to the hitch. Ah. Sigh of relief. The trailer was fine, just cocked at an awkward angle off the side of the road. But still upright, still connected. It could have been so much worse.

Absentmindedly, Henry dabbed at his leg where the drink had spilled and went around to the passenger side to right the boxes. Out of the corner of his eye, he saw a flash of the deer in the distance.

Pure white.

An albino, he guessed. *Damn thing could have killed me. I guess that's why they call it the Wastelands. Taken over by damn ghostly deer.*

He looked to the woods. *And who knows what else.*

He gently, cautiously eased the car back on the road, slowly straightening out the hitch and trailer into a straight line. Back on the road bed, all lined up, Henry got back out to double-check the hitch and such.

Everything seemed okay. He breathed a formally deep breath and thanked his lucky stars and any god who might be listening or cared in the slightest.

Hey, to all of you, thanks.

He flicked his eyes heavenward, just in case.

The last few hours though the northern expanse of the Wastelands was uneventful, and civilization—he gave a bitter laugh at that word—started to encroach on the wild and barren landscape. Small towns at first, then skirting the edge of a major megapolis, the last one this far north. He had to stop once to fuel up on liquid hydrogen. It was probably overkill, but he pulled on a special prosthetic face mask just in case. It didn't look like a mask, just like a normal person. But it was specially designed to confuse the recognition algorithms. It was also highly illegal. He didn't tarry.

Finally, just as dawn reluctantly crawled up and over the fractured horizon, he saw the signs for the town. Newthington was just up ahead. Street lights and guide beacons gave a warm, familiar, welcoming glow to the small town; an island of convenience and comfort after the abandoned, indifferent brutality of the wasted regions.

But he avoided that and instead skirted the very rim of the town, staying well away from the center, to the farthest edge where Weatherly Hall lay waiting. The real estate agent, an unnaturally perky woman named Gloria, had sent him the keys via courier service. Well, not directly to him, of course—that would be too easily traceable. But through enough freight forwarders and misdirection, he eventually got the keys and the deed to this magnificent anachronism.

What the hell am I doing? He wound his way past desolate fields to foothills where the mansion lay.

He flirted with doubt for a minute. Really, this was insane. He'd bought a huge, barely-functional estate with no staff. There wasn't a lot of money left for renovations, and he certainly didn't want to do anything showy anyway. He couldn't be seen as the "new rich guy" in town flashing a lot of cash about.

Shit, the state goons would be on me in a heartbeat. Mine. My last, probably.

No, anything that needed fixing, he needed to manage himself. Anything he needed to live, to survive, he needed to do himself. He was on his own.

In a world dominated by interconnectedness, by total surveillance, total awareness, analyzed to death by AI, by low-level state officers, by your own damn nosy neighbors anxious to score points, he was the anachronism.

He was on his own.

Two

THE SKY WAS AN EVEN, DULL GRAY. A featureless backdrop to the faded green and unenthusiastic dark red and yellow leaves. It wasn't bad until the wind whipped up; a cold, piercing, stony hand seizing your very bones. At least the wind was fresh and carried away some of the heavy scent of damp leaves and seasonal beginnings of rot and decay.

Yeah, I'm in a great mood. Henry kicked at a pile of about-to-be rotting leaves. *Well, I wanted to be alone—I think I got that part right. This is about as alone as it gets.*

He had gotten out of the car to unlock the gates: big, heavy, ironwork affairs. Beautifully made, they opened and closed by hand only. There were no hydraulics, no motors, nothing. Parting the piles of leaves, he fumbled with the keys—actual metal, mechanical keys—until he found the one that fit the old-fashioned padlock. The hinges creaked with age but did the job. He left the gates open, for now, and drove up the long, leaf-filled gravel driveway.

More leaves than gravel. He drove slowly and tried to pick out the road from the forest floor. Trees were close on each side and in some places met each other to form a canopy above. Most of the leaves were gone now, but Henry noted that it would get pretty dark and closed-in along this road in the summer months. The road wound its way rising through the woods and finally out into a clearing up at the top of the property. One last turn and Henry saw the house proper.

And what a house it was.

Holy shit.

His eyes widened as the mansion loomed into sight, and he tried to take it all in at once. The images he'd seen of it were impressive, but up close, it was downright massive. He slowed and made his way around the circular part of the drive in front of the house, past some decidedly creepy statuary, under the watchful eye of even creepier gargoyles up on the roofline.

He looked up at those and wondered why architects of olden times would put these horrible visages on otherwise beautiful, ornate buildings. Apparently, the goal was to scare away evil spirits. He winked and smiled up at the snarling drain spouts and wished them success.

Those weeping women statues bordering the driveway, though, that was another matter. He shook his head; no idea what that was about. He might haul those down to the basement for storage at some point. Walking past those figures on a dark and misty morning would be… unpleasant. He'd look for an outside entrance to the basement when he had a chance. But first things first.

He got out of the car, opened the rear trailer doors, and sighed at the hasty, jammed-up fortress of bulging fiberboard boxes and snarled packing tape. How much of this junk did he *really* need? Old books, some clothes, basic pots and pans. The stuff of life. He'd thrown out the awards from work, the stupid gag gifts from innumerable Christmases and birthdays. Old memories of childhood were long gone—he'd ditched those at least a couple of moves ago. This was supposed to be his pared-down version of life, only what fit in a small DIY-Haul trailer. He'd paid cash to own a used one, not rent. It wasn't properly licensed; he was gambling that he wouldn't be noticed. And he'd kept it small. Henry tried not to hoard material possessions.

Digital data and archives, though, that was another story entirely. Knowledge. That was his passion. He searched, he collected, he hung on to every precious bit he could. You had to, once you found it. Stuff could disappear off the nets or from libraries and did. Regularly. News, facts, history, it didn't matter. Nothing was permanent, not even truth. Bits were erased, paper was burned, libraries shuttered. It had become a sort of global amnesia, forgetting and rewriting whatever didn't fit with the current narrative of power. So the handful of crystal memory wafers in his pocket were more valuable to him than anything in the trailer. And much more dangerous to have. Too dangerous to have in the megapolis.

Despite the attraction of the digital, one had to bow to the necessities of life in the real. Cooking, sleeping, clothing, bathing, and all that. That took up real space and couldn't be reduced to a bunch of qubits on a crystal wafer.

Henry walked up the wide stone stairs to the front door. It was massive; aged oak, perhaps. He raised a hand, ran it along the iron-like carved grain of the door. Solid. Like rock. He pushed gently; there was no give, no yielding. He fumbled again with the mechanical keys, heard a series of clicks and squeaks as the lock relented, and pushed the door open. It swung wide, grudgingly, hinges complaining the whole way. A gust of wind exchanged the air in the entrance hallway; it was as if the house woke up and took a deep breath.

Nonsense. He dismissed the thought. *Houses don't breathe. They're just damn big boxes. Hope this one is sealed tight against the cold.*

Time to start moving into this big box.

He started dutifully hauling his stuff in through the massive oaken door into the entrance hall, occasionally marveling at the stained-glass side lights and transom. It really had been a beautiful property once. *And still was,* underneath the grime and disrepair.

That, I can fix. One bit at a time, slowly but persistently.

The black and white diamond tile floor had a finesse, a quiet quality that you just didn't see these days. Even before the war, it wasn't common. Back when people still built new houses, any decorative parts and materials were usually mass-produced and imported from the Asia/Pacific region. Hand-crafted, skilled artisanal work was practically non-existent even then. Now? Unheard of.

But then, back in that time, the rich could afford to hire the exceptionally skilled. The images Henry had seen of Weatherly Hall showed unusual attention to detail. Hand-woven fabric on the walls, hand-carved, highly polished woodwork, stair rails, molding, you name it. The place was a damn work of art. A treasure.

And a mess.

Henry noticed two big piles of… what, soot? Ash? Dirt? One pile lay on either side of the front door but in the hall by a few feet. He looked up and around; there was no obvious vent or opening where the dirt may have come from. Maybe it just gathered in the circular vortex wind patterns of the hall? He looked past the hall, into the great ballroom, trying to figure out any sort of pattern. It really didn't make any sense.

Better sweep this up before I track it everywhere. He went back out to the trailer and poked around until he found the broom and dustpan he'd brought. It was a little bit of an affectation, using something so old-fashioned and manual instead of a vacuum bot. But Henry was serious about reducing the amount of tech in his life. Back in the hallway, he swept up the piles of ash in the two corners and was headed back outside to dump the dustpan when he noticed something odd.

There was a design in the middle of the entrance floor.

Henry hadn't seen it at first, but now that he was sweeping and looking around a little more closely, there, smack in the middle, expertly cut in into the tile, was the figure of a deer. A white, albino deer against a black tile background, inset in the overall diamond pattern.

Huh. He had thought white deer were rare. *Guess not. Must be common around these parts.* He dumped the ash outside and began hauling boxes from the trailer. Henry stacked the boxes tight there in the hall, planning on unpacking them later.

Maybe. He was standing there in the hall, contemplating the light—still gray and diffuse—coming through the stained glass transom over the entrance when he heard a door slam upstairs.

Shit. I'm not alone.

The front door had been locked, but who knows how many other doors existed and in what state. Or if there were any unexpected openings—a broken window, damaged rooms open to the elements, that sort of thing.

His heart raced, and the hairs on the back of his neck raised at attention.

No one should be here.

No one had been here in at least fifteen years, according to perky Gloria the real estate agent.

Henry tried to climb the main staircase—a magnificent affair—quietly, to the second story. But "quiet" was next to impossible. The stairs creaked and moaned at the intrusion. He looked down the long hall to the right; to the left. He called out in a surprisingly weak and halting voice, "Is someone there? Hello?"

No surprise, there was no answer. Just the wind outside, slapping the house to see if it was awake. He looked down at the floor in front of him.

Dust.

Dust on the floor, thick and uniform. No one had been up this way, not lately. He looked up and down the long hallway again, closer this time.

Undisturbed dust.

And silent. Whatever door slammed must have been from a combination of opening the front door and an opportunistic gust of wind. No one had been here, no one else *was* here. Just him. He breathed a half-sigh of relief but kept a more cautious ear open for anything else unexpected. At least he was certain no one could sneak up on him. With these creaky floorboards, there would be no sneaking in this house.

He creaked back down to the main story and closed the massive front door. *That's why they call it Weatherly Hall.* He had first figured it was built by a Mr. Weatherly, but not so. It was actually built by one Mr. Ferguson. Not quite as poetic. Instead of being named for the owner, the "Weatherly" Hall name was quite literal. Perched up on the highest hill in the area, it caught more than its share of wind, weather, and storm.

So, there you go.

After properly securing the front door, he headed back to the kitchen, which was through the grand ballroom and then a small passageway to the right. The kitchen was surprisingly small, with a stunningly out-dated stove that looked like it dated from the early twen-tieth century, the 1930s, maybe? Henry took a closer look at it. Yes, a genuine antique gas stove. He wondered if it even worked. Plumbing pipes ran loosely along the walls, clearly a later addition to the property. Henry bet those were going to rattle like a pair of maracas from Mexamerica.

But still, it was a larger kitchen then he'd ever had. Once he unpacked and got things set up, he planned on making fantastic meals from local vegetables and such. But for now, he'd just open a can of beans. Henry went back out front, dug through the larger boxes until he found the beans and the microwave, carried it back and plugged it into what looked like the *only* electrical outlet in the kitchen. One outlet, and an old-fashioned one at that. Power only, no data.

Well, that's what I wanted, isn't it? It wasn't much, but it worked. So he had plain old working electrical service, at least.

He ate the now-warmed beans, washed them down with the remains of the coffeesynth, and finished empty-ing the trailer. Once that was done, almost everything he owned was stacked in the magnificent entrance hallway.

He got the last box out of the car, from the front seat. A handful of disposable, illegal, unregistered burner cell phones in a shielded Faraday box. He hoped he'd never need them—these phones were for dire emergencies only. In case the house caught fire, or he needed a cash am-bulance, that sort of thing. He'd need to put the box someplace far out of sight, where no one would stumble across it by accident. He went back to the kitchen and wrestled the heavy iron grate loose from the bottom of the stove. There was a storage space there—*God knows what for.* He shoved the Faraday box way in the back, stuffed some canned goods in front of it, and wrestled the heavy door shut.

No one's going to find that easily, even with a scanner.

Henry ambled out from the kitchen through the large ballroom to the front, the floors creaking loudly as he went. The ballroom had a magnificent, polished wood floor, carved woodwork, and display alcoves throughout. Some had figures in them, some were empty. Dust and spiderwebs were everywhere. He made it back to the entry hall, looked at the pile, and sighed.

Maybe I'll explore a bit first. Starting with the bed-rooms. The house was listed as "partially furnished," and his inquiries suggested that some bedroom furniture was included. He had a sleeping bag packed just in case.

He climbed the giant staircase—slowly, this time, not in a panic—and looked down both long hallways.

This might take a while.

Henry decided to check out the left side of the house first. *Would this be the east wing? Or west?* The hallway was windowless, so he couldn't easily tell where the sun was. In fact, he had to admit this house probably didn't get a lot of light, even on sunny days. He'd have to check the compass at some point; that might help him keep the house straight in his head.

The long hall stretched out in front of him, two doors on both sides, offset. The floor wasn't all on one level; there was a two-step stair along the way, and niches and alcoves along the walls as well.

Some architect had a lot of fun with this. He opened the first door he found, on his right. It was like a smaller version of the massive front door: oak, carved, with hinges that complained loudly and bitterly at being rousted from their rest. He stepped inside with an extra-large creak from the floorboards.

It was a decent-sized room but not large enough for a bed. A dressing room perhaps? The plans he'd seen had hinted at that. He walked in and looked out the large window that faced the rear of the estate. The wall that stretched from the hallway to the outside wall had sliding doors in the center. He pulled them open and walked into a *very* large bedroom.

Two large windows and a larger bay window looked out to the rear. There was no bed in here, but clearly this was meant to be a bedroom. Dirty outlines on the walls showed where artwork was once hung. Henry walked over to the bay window and looked out. It was still morning, and the weak sun was lighting up the front of the house, not here. *So the rear rooms face west.* He went back out through the dressing room into the hallway. Offset from that door was another; he went in to find an even larger dressing room.

This room had a large bay window facing the… *south*, he reckoned. Opposite the bay window was a set of doors. He opened them, surprised to find a large closet. He backed up and saw the doors opposite the entry door he had come in. He went through.

This was a magnificent bedroom. *Must be the master?* The bed was certainly large enough, and high enough. He wondered if he'd need a step stool just to climb onboard the mattress. He also idly wondered how many mice and critters might be living in it. Henry walked past the bed and drew open the heavy, dark drapes from the bay window facing the front of the house. Thin gray light invaded the room, casting shadows on the thick dust. The dust was winning, for now. The broom and dustpan he'd brought wouldn't cut it. He'd need to vacuum. A lot. He really didn't want to have to resort to a vacuum bot, but these first few rooms were huge, and he hadn't even seen most of the rest of the house yet.

In the front corner of the bedroom was a small round turret of a room, overlooking the front of the house and the driveway. He poked his head in.

How many rooms does this place even have?

Free, safe, alone. That was the plan. Despite the "going it alone" idea, he started to think that just maybe he'd have to find some help. Even with a bot, the sheer scale of the place was daunting. This one bedroom was nearly as large as his entire apartment had been.

He brushed off a large, overstuffed chair by the front window, raising a small, perturbed cloud, and let loose an epic, bone-shaking sneeze. *A cleaning person? At some point. I'm not giving up yet.* He sat, sniffled, and took in the view. From here, he could see the circular driveway, the creepy statuary, and the long drive disappearing into the woods on its way down the mountain to the gates out by the main road.

Only one way in, easily watched from any of the rooms on the front side. Good.

There was an ornate end table over in the corner, Henry got up and dragged it across the floor. It made a loud, unpleasant noise as it scraped. He hoped he wasn't leaving marks.

But here, then. This would be a fine spot to settle into. He pictured himself in a luxurious bathrobe, sipping tea in the elegant Victorian—*I think?*—arm chair, a snack at hand on the elaborately carved end table.

He ran his hand along the dusty top. *Yeah, this could work.* But so much cleaning to be done—not just the dust and vacuuming but the grime. He looked closely at the walls, which featured a diamond-pattern of blue and green silk.

How do you even clean upholstered walls?

Henry left the bedroom and headed down the creaking hall, past where he came in, to the next bedroom, this one facing the rear of the house. It featured a similarly grumpy door, and was almost the same size as the first bedroom, with a dressing room first, then entry to the bedroom itself.

Hah, maybe they are all "masters." Again he went to the large window and pulled back the drapes. From here, he could see the field at the rear of the house and the woods falling away down the side of the mountain.

Back out through the dressing room, he closed the bedroom door and looked back down the long hall, past where he had come up on the stairs, and thought he saw something.

Motion. At the end of the hall. A figure.

Henry sucked his breath in hard, felt his back muscles clamp up tighter than his bones could bear, his stomach joining in and forcing bile up into his mouth. He froze, didn't move.

Shit! I'm not alone after all!

"Who's there!" he shouted as an accusation, not a question.

The figure didn't move.

"Stop. Don't move. Who are you!" Henry demanded and advanced slowly down the hall. The figure wavered, looking formless and shadowy. Against the advice of the voice in his head, he broke into a slight jog and ran toward the figure, which wavered and fluttered even more as he did.

What the actual fuck? That one was a question.

Henry passed the stairs and was halfway down the hallway when he saw clearly enough to realize what it was.

A large, framed, antique, over-sized mirror in a massive frame had been placed at the end of the hall. The lighting was just dim and murky enough to have made a spectral vision of his own reflection.

Oh, for fuck's sake. Henry slumped against the wall, let out a breath, and quickly took a deeper one. Running terror sprints was not his style.

New house jitters, that's all. There was so much to take in here, so many unfamiliar items. *Who the hell even owns giant mirrors like that?* He scowled at his distorted reflection and decided to fix this problem right now. He grabbed an edge of the frame and started to turn the mirror around, to face the wall.

It was surprisingly heavy.

Henry got it about halfway around, a few groaning, creaking centimeters at a time, and gave up. *Good enough. At least this way it won't scare the living shit out of me every time I'm in the hallway.*

He had gone down a few stairs to this level; there was a set of narrow and twisted passages and much smaller bedrooms. The first several bedrooms were definitely the largest, and each room was a little different—the number and shape of the windows, the height of the floor, some had steps up and down, some were on the same plane.

Those first few seemed mostly furnished, but the smaller bedrooms in the twisty section were completely empty. Unused, by the looks of it. Henry tried to spend some time in each room, not just have a quick look around, but to really try and *feel* what the room was like, to appreciate its unique view and placement, and its own oddities of layout, alcoves, niches, and so on.

There was a narrow, rickety-looking staircase in this section, too. *Servants' staircase?* That would make sense and explain the smaller quarters. Or maybe these rooms were for younger family members.

He made his way back out to the landing and saw that the balcony extended all the way around the edges of the ballroom below. He walked down one side to a door, found another small lobby, bathroom, and bedroom, plus the stairs up to the third floor. *Next time, maybe.*

Still a little out of breath from his fright, he headed back down the stairs to the kitchen, to sit, to catch his breath. Henry weaved past the tower of his crap in the front hallway and regretted that he hadn't thrown out more than he did.

Probably should at least set up the kitchen, make something for lunch. It had been at least a few hours since the beans and coffee, and that hadn't really satisfied.

A blast of wind rocked the house, and it groaned. Henry stiffened. *Okay, can't let the house noises freak you out. It's not like the house is... haunted or anything.*

Of course, it wasn't haunted. There was no such thing as ghosts. After his mom died, he'd really hoped there was such a thing as ghosts, or spirits of the newly departed. Something. He missed her. He tried, read a bunch of half-baked occult articles, burned candles and incense, but nothing worked. He never saw her ghost.

Because there is no such thing.

Was there?

Were ghosts real? Or Bigfoot, for that matter? Panda bears? Whales? Many said that these elements of the supernatural and cryptozoology were real, that these creatures once roamed the Earth. Others said they were fake; nothing more than promo stunts for movies in the late 1800s and early 1900s. No one knew for sure anymore. The tapestry of history was torn and threadbare, patched with both tattered cloth and with trash.

These creatures don't seem to exist now. Maybe they did, then. Maybe they never did.

Henry convinced himself there were no such thing as ghosts, but at the same time felt he might need a breather. He hadn't planned on heading into town this early for supplies, but he didn't really have anything to eat for lunch except a repeat of breakfast beans, and that held no allure.

He grabbed his coat, locked the front door behind him, and headed to his car. As he unhitched the trailer, he wondered where in town he might be able to find an old-fashioned china tea set.

Three

THERE WAS A MAN BY THE SIDE OF THE ROAD. An old man, bearded and hunched. He was on the edge of what looked like one large garden—or many smaller, connected ones—next to a driveway that ran up through the gardens and disappeared in a large hedge.

He waved as Henry drove past. Henry thought a moment, slowed down, and reversed the car.

Might as well get to meet the neighbors straight away.

He lowered the side window and leaned out. "Hello!"

The man straightened up and leaned on a long garden tool, some sort of shovel, hoe, or rake thing. Henry wasn't sure. The man was wearing something on his head—a peaked turban. Pretty brave to wear anything like that out in the open. At least, it would have been back in the city. Maybe not as much of a problem out here. That was a good sign.

"Hello," the man said, and nodded up the road toward the gate. "You have come from Weatherly?"

Henry hesitated just a moment; he needed to get his cover story straight in his head. "Yes, the mansion. I'll be staying there a while. Got hired to caretake the place by some big company. Don't know why, but they're paying me to babysit the house, spruce it up, that sort of thing." He tried not to blurt it all out at once. Failed. Nervously, he tried to change the subject. "Little late in the year for gardening, isn't it?"

The old man just smiled back, radiating a pervasive calm. He looked at the sprawling gardens in front of the hedge, and replied, "Oh, there's always something needs tending, every season, really. I've got some late bloomers to work with, and the beds here need to be readied for spring. Always something." He looked back at Henry. "My name is Anahat Sukhjodh Singh. You may call me Anah; that's what my friends call me."

"Hi, Anah. I'm…" Henry hesitated just a fraction here. "Friends call me J." That was only a little misleading. His friends from school called him Hank. It wouldn't do to go by his middle name, Jamal; that was too ethic. But J would be okay; it was nondescript, forgettable. He wanted to hurry the conversation past this part. "You live here? There's a house?" Henry pointed to the hedge.

"Oh, yes," Anah replied. "In the house. Up the driveway. Long driveway. Large house. Not as large as your Weatherly, of course, but big enough for me, my wife, and daughters. But I know Weatherly well. My mother, she used to cook for the big parties at Weatherly Hall, back in the day. Such a huge kitchen, and that massive stove. It was said you could cook an entire ox in it at once!"

"Parties?" Henry asked.

"Oh, yes, yes." Anah nodded vigorously, his turban bobbing. "Grand parties, not every day, of course, but often enough. It was such a place of joy and laughter." He looked wistful. "Standing tall in defense against the weather of the world." He fell silent.

Henry couldn't help his curiosity. "What happened, exactly? I mean, the house still stands and is great shape, but it's clearly been abandoned for a long time."

Anah looked up the road. "Long time, yes," he said quietly, then turned back to Henry. "Oh, the usual reasons. Mrs. Morris passed—her family owned the mansion for many, many years, and it was Mr. and Mrs. Morris who hosted the parties. Then the war came, and, well." He stopped, clearly uncomfortable. "Are you headed into town?" Now it was Anah's turn to redirect the conversation. Right back to Henry.

"Town, right. Yeah, I need to find a grocer, pick up some supplies. Maybe some dishes, that sort of thing," Henry replied. In the back of his mind, he was still thinking of picking up a delicate china tea set.

"Stay right on the main road; you'll go right past Rudder's General Store. You cannot miss it." Anah waved up the road.

"Sounds easy enough." Henry smiled. "Well, it was nice meeting you. I better get going."

Anah waved, smiled his serene smile, and silently moved through the field. Henry pulled away down the main road into town.

———

Family. Anah seemed to have it made—wife, kids, happily tending his garden. Henry shook his head in silent disbelief. His own family was far from such an idyll. His dad was, well…

Dad was an asshole, Henry had to admit.

Henry's father was a firm believer in the "hierarchy." He demanded a strict hierarchy of the world: God over man, strong over weak, white man over all. That seemed inconsistent at first; while Henry's father was pasty white, Henry's mom was, in his father's words, "exotic," sharing Henry's khaki-and-olive colored skin.

Mom let Dad think what he wanted, but she clearly ran the household. But Dad never knew she was really in charge. He thought he was God almighty himself.

The rest of the family disagreed.

When his father died, Henry was relieved. Guilty for feeling that way, but relieved, nonetheless.

His mom had died first, when they were still young, and his sister hadn't spoken to Henry in… He had to stop and think. Years, now, at least. Years. He couldn't remember why they stopped talking to each other.

But here was the store. Henry turned in and parked.

———

Rudder's was a little more primitive than Henry would have liked. A small, whitewashed concrete rectangle with a lot of bare shelves. Some sad produce and canned goods that may have been war surplus. Possibly not even the most recent war. But it did have hardware, some tools, and supplies, in addition to grocery staples. He picked up a couple of basics: hammer, pliers, wire cutters, a spool of electrical wire, and a couple of outlet boxes. He was sure he'd need to pop in a few extra of those. More light would probably help too, and he was in luck here: Rudder's had a supply of old-fashioned, non-networked lightbulbs.

The young checkout clerk nodded as Henry came up to the counter but was clearly more interested in whatever was playing on both earpieces than in chatting, which suited Henry just fine. He paid in cash tokens and headed out to his car.

Rudder's General Store might have been part of a strip mall once, when such things were popular. Now there were just a few smallish, disconnected buildings sharing a parking lot. Near Rudder's, but not connected, was a bar. The faded paint whispered the name *The Grumpy Yorkie*. It wasn't open yet, but Henry made a mental note to check it out some evening. Might be a good way to socialize in a low-key, largely anonymous setting. Henry was slightly worried that he might go a little crazy all alone in the house.

Well, I wanted to be left alone, he mused as he loaded a few small bags of groceries into his car. He had to buy the bags; that was a new twist. He hadn't needed grocery bags in the city, where his groceries were delivered. *Alone, but on my own terms. I can come visit with folks if I want, when I want.* It would all work out, he was sure.

He started the car and was about to turn to go back to Weatherly Hall, but on impulse, turned the other way to head farther into town. _Just to see._ He didn't want to go all the way into the town center but was curious as to what else lay here near the edge that might be useful.

More buildings, cheap housing, rundown stores, vacant lots; the usual. He was about to turn back when he saw a small blue road sign that read *Town Library.* He turned in and followed it.

It was clearly old. Many towns up this way had old libraries, but "old" in that context usually meant mid-twentieth century, when concrete and faux-modern brutalism was in style. Those had been mostly torn down or abandoned. But this, this was something different. It might have been from Weatherly Hall's era or shortly thereafter. Early 1900s, 1930s maybe? Henry wasn't sure, but it was a three-story brick building, ornate, old-fashioned, and a bit on the dark and creepy side. He looked up. *Yup, gargoyles again.* It did not help the look.

But Henry loved libraries, in general, and old, forgotten ones in particular. His passion for arcane, forgotten lore wasn't confined to his precious memory crystals. Real, physical libraries were increasingly rare. And exciting. He parked and strode up the wide marble stairs. The front doors were modern and glass, but once through, he was in another world.

Three stories of book stacks, filled with actual, paper books. Ancient, forgotten books that no one had bothered to burn. The scent of paper, bookbinding, and glue, musty with age, was downright intoxicating.

Henry straightened and let out a long, low breath. This was an incredible find. He walked over to the nearest stack and ran his finger along the spines of a couple of the closest books. The last time his stomach had this many butterflies, he'd been on a date.

A gravelly, rusty voice, as ancient as the library itself, perhaps, called over to him, "Can I help you, sir?"

Henry looked over and stepped out of the stack's aisle into the main hall of the library to see who it was. She was an old woman in a green dress, half-moon spectacles hanging from a chain around her neck, and she was right there in front of him. Henry startled; he hadn't seen her approach.

"Hi, er, yes. Yes, you can help me; that'd be great." He stumbled over the words. He hadn't planned this part out.

The woman nodded curtly. "What are you looking for today?"

Henry thought quickly. "Well, a job, actually. Or even just a chance to volunteer," he amended, with a wave of his hands. "I didn't know this library was here, and well, it's really quite impressive!" He failed to contain his enthusiasm and only *barely* was able to suppress something uncomfortably close to a giggle.

She picked up her spectacles and perched them on the end of her nose, giving Henry a more thorough scan up and down. "I haven't seen you in town before," she said suspiciously. "Are you new here?"

"Yes, very much so," Henry replied. "I just got here yesterday, in fact. My name's J." He bowed slightly, hand to heart, as was the custom in the megapolis. "I was hired to take care of the Weatherly Hall estate, clean it up, spruce it up a little."

"Were you now?" She cocked her head, intrigued at this idea.

"I guess I just love old buildings." He smiled and waved at the towering stacks. "But I love libraries even more. I'd be delighted to help out here, if you need it."

"Of course," she said. "I'm Esmeralda. Esmeralda Vega. I'm the head librarian here. Well," she smiled, "to be fair, I'm the *only* librarian here. I could absolutely use some help. It would have to be on a volunteer basis. I barely have enough budget to heat this place in the winter."

"That's fine, Ms. Vega," Henry replied. "I'm just looking for something useful to do to fill the hours when I'm not taking care of Weatherly." He looked down the hall at the stacks. "This is a fantastic collection. I can't remember the last time I've seen such a large one. Even the main branch in the capital of New Yorkland isn't so big, I think. And I haven't found a library in Weatherly Hall at all, yet."

Esmeralda followed his gaze and sighed. "Yes, it's unusually large. It's not as broad as you might like, though. Many of these works are related to mining and early industrial-age manufacturing. That's what Newthington was known for, in its day. And in a way, this *is* Weatherly Hall's library." Henry looked back at her with a quizzical expression. "Originally, many of these books were at Weatherly, but the Fergusons donated money to the town to build this library in the 1930s, at the height of the first depression, and then donated all the books, with an endowment to add more to the collections over the years."

Henry whistled low and thoughtfully. "Wow. That's incredible by itself, but how did it all survive the Second Civil War? So many libraries were torched, so many books burned, it's really rare to find any large collections anymore."

Esmeralda shrugged. "Luck. Apathy. I think the townspeople at the time considered these books to be boring, or at least contained nothing to challenge their truths."

They both fell silent for a moment.

"Truth" was one of those words that people tended to avoid in polite company. There was nothing actually wrong with it, certainly no formal policies against it as word or concept. But it carried the same weight as mentioning a dead relative; a loved one lost at sea, or dead to a terrible, grisly accident.

The truth, most felt, died in the mid-21st century. No one set out to kill the truth, to deliberately murder it. Its death was largely accidental. It was smothered, buried under an unprecedented avalanche of bullshit. Like the ancient cities of Pompeii and Herculaneum, everything was lost. Afterward, you could see only the outlines of history. When Vesuvius erupted, the ash filled every empty space, obliterating the people and the landscape, but leaving holes—3D outlines of the bodies themselves.

In the post-Second Civil War history, there were holes where the bullshit wasn't. Areas that the bullshit traced, outlined, and filled right up against but wasn't able to penetrate. The holes in the bullshit—that was the truth, or all that was left of it.

At least, that's all that Henry had ever had to work with. But here, in this forgotten information enclave, was perhaps some remnants of pre-war truth, untouched by the avalanche of bullshit that had so successfully smothered the world. He couldn't believe his luck.

Esmeralda gave Henry a quick tour of the main parts of the library—there was a small attic and basement that weren't included in that—and they worked out a simple schedule at first. If he proved reliable, she'd let him open and close on a few days to give her time for errands and family.

She bowed to him as Henry was leaving.

"Thank you so much for this," Henry said. "You really don't know what this means to me."

"Perhaps I do." Esmeralda smiled, turned, and went back inside.

Henry came up over the rise just before Anah's sprawling gardens and hedge, and sure enough, Anah was still out in front, farther up now, still close to the road, but in another part of the garden, poking at weeds.

Henry slowed and pulled onto the shoulder, lowering the window on that side.

"Ah, Mr. J! So nice to see you again. I trust your mission into town was successful?"

"My… oh, yes, yes, indeed, thank you. I picked up some tools and supplies from Rudder's, and enough for a late lunch now, I guess."

Anah smiled as he always did. "Very good. Well, if there's anything I can do for you, anything at all, please do call on me. I'm usually right here." His smile widened, if that were possible at all.

"You're very kind, thank you," Henry said with genuine gratitude. Helpful friends were rare in this world. "And any time you'd like to come and hang out at Weatherly, please feel free—it's not like I'm cramped or anything." Henry laughed, and Anah laughed as well, his eyes crinkling.

Anah pulled on his beard thoughtfully. "Yes, yes, of course. I have fond memories of my mother cooking feasts in that wondrous kitchen, guests drinking and dancing well into the night."

Henry ventured into more personal territory. "Your turban—you're Sikh, right? I didn't think your people drank. Just curious, no offense."

Anah shook his head. "Oh, none taken at all, my friend. You are new, questions are welcome. Yes, my family is Sikh. We believe in helping." He gestured up the road. "Helping neighbors, helping humanity, helping wherever we can. And you are correct, we do not drink alcohol. But," he wagged his finger, "our way is our way.

Our path is our path. Your path is yours alone, and I would never presume to force others to drink or not drink because of the nature of *my* own path. It is not our way."

Religious but not zealots. Henry made a mental *huh*. "Okay, I see. Thank you. I've never met a Sikh before, so I'm sure I'll have all kinds of stupid questions. Please forgive my ignorance and any insult ahead of time, and again, if there's anything I, or Weatherly Hall, can do for you, please just ask."

At this, Anah tilted his head back and laughed most heartily. "Thank you so much for your kindness. I will certainly remember that. And as for offense, honest questions never offer offense. Please ask as you will."

Henry smiled back, almost dazed with wonder. He'd never met anyone like Anah. So many people these days were quick to offend—often with violent consequences. Don't ask, don't talk about heritage, political views, who you supported in the war—none of that was considered polite. Yet here was a turban-wearing Sikh, proud of his heritage, his beliefs, taking no offense despite what Henry felt were probably very ignorant and offensive questions, and offering friendship to basically a complete stranger.

"Okay, I will!" Henry promised. "But right now, I better get my groceries back."

"Of course," Anah said with what was apparently a completely consistent serenity.

Henry drove back to Weatherly. The weeping women statuary really had to go, he thought again.

He parked and decided to take a quick look for an entrance to the basement, so he could haul the statues into storage. Nothing obvious at the front of the house; he walked around to the left all the way back to the greenhouse corner and around back. There were patios and entry doors to the main level, but nothing that looked basement-related. Back to the front of the house he went, past the entry porch in the other direction, and saw what might have been a small delivery chute of some kind.

Coal chute? Or firewood. Maybe supplies.

Henry wasn't sure what it would have been used for, but it was definitely too small for a person—or a large weeping woman statue. Back to the front door, he fumbled with the mechanical locks again and walked into the hallway.

That's weird. He looked down, and there were two piles of ash, or soot, in the corners again.

The same piles he had cleaned up this morning. He looked more closely at the walls, the floor, and the distant ceiling, but there was no obvious opening or source. *Where is that coming from?* He frowned in frustration. There was plenty of cleaning and repair to do; he didn't need any mysterious dirt on top of it all.

He'd left the broom and dustpan by the front door, so he once again swept up the piles and dumped them outside, then unloaded his groceries into the pantry and the small, ancient refrigerator.

He decided to put on some music, with a dedicated high-res music player—not connected to any network, no streaming or tracking, all local storage. He was in a mood for The Eagles, a popular mid-twentieth century band from what was then California, and made himself a sandwich for a very late lunch.

As he sat and ate, listening to the mellifluous tones of such classic music, he thought about The Eagles and about that near-paradise vision of last-century California. *Maybe that was the pinnacle of pre-Second Civil War civilization.* Environmentally conscious, respectful of natural variations in race, sexuality, gender, age…

He'd sometimes thought about emigrating to Ecotopia from New Yorkland, but after the war, they had very strict immigration quotas. You had to have something very valuable to offer their economy in order to get citizenship there. And Henry felt he just didn't. Nothing that he could admit to publicly, anyway. Well, things that he couldn't admit to here in New Yorkland. But in Ecotopia? They very likely had different sensibilities when it came to archival data and long-lost knowledge. But he'd never had the courage to test that theory. Not yet, anyway.

Henry finished his sandwich and looked at the expanse of kitchen wall behind him. Something that Anah said echoed in his head.

Anah said his mother had cooked here, for the big feasts and parties they used to have here. But looking around, this kitchen just wasn't all that big. Certainly not in scale with the rest of the house. And there was no massive stove—Anah had mentioned something about a massive stove. But this stove wasn't massive at all; it was a small, gas-powered affair. There was nothing like a massive stove here, at least not in *this* kitchen.

Maybe there was another?

Henry decided to take a closer look.

Four

HENRY STEPPED OUT OF THE KITCHEN into the passageway. To his left was the small hall with the servants' stairs that led to the grand ballroom and the entrance hall. Ahead of him was an opening to a large space with floor-to-ceiling windows facing the back of the property. He poked his head in. A massive, long table dominated the room, and hard wooden chairs were lined up against the walls. *Dining room, apparently.*

Back in the passageway, he followed the twists and turns past a storeroom and into a small bedroom. Unlike the bedrooms he'd seen upstairs, this one had no dressing room, but it did have a very ornate door with bars over the glass. He opened the door to find a closet filled with velvet-lined open shelves and locking drawers. *Some sort of safe or strong room.* That would make this the bedroom of the head servant. Butler or steward, he wasn't sure what the differences were. But clearly this was the guy who slept guarding the family silver and jewels. The strong room was empty of all of that now, of course. *"Partially furnished" apparently doesn't include heirloom silver.* There was an even smaller, winding, and rickety-looking staircase for the head steward's use opposite the strong room.

Henry backed out and, passing the entrance to the kitchen again, went all the way into the dining room this time, accompanied by the usual chorus of loud, creaking floorboards. He saw the magnificent flagstone patio outside and began to appreciate how much of a party house this must have been in its day. He continued on to the adjacent drawing room, again with large windows—and an even larger bay window—and then through to a smaller drawing room with an outside door. He stuck his head out and found the greenhouse.

Most of the glass was still intact but not all. The remains of the jungle inside had spilled out and grappled with the encroaching jungle outside, and all smelled of damp, rich earth. He took a step into the greenhouse. It would take some work, but clearly things could grow here, even in this far northern climate.

Given the state of the sad vegetables at Rudder's market, this might a good backup. Henry imagined growing his own vegetables here, supporting himself truly off the grid, when he felt a sudden sharp prick and icy cold hand on his shoulder.

"Fuck!" he screamed and whipped around in a startled panic, flinging the squirrel off his shoulder. The terrified squirrel skittered along a long low shelf, through the loose dirt, before disappearing out through a hole to the comparative safety of the outside world. Henry bent over, hands on knees, trying to catch his breath, which was coming in rough, racking gasps at the moment.

Just a squirrel. Just a squirrel. Settle down. You're okay. He shook his head as if to clear it, straightened up, and realized his hands were shaking. Henry took a deep breath and closed the greenhouse door tightly behind him. Gardening would have to wait.

Moving on back through the small drawing room toward the front of the house, Henry found the break-fast room, or at least a smaller, informal dining room. It featured a very large bay window, on the same side of the house as the greenhouse. Henry realized that was the southern exposure, so probably was one of the most well-lit areas in an otherwise pretty dark house. Next to the breakfast room was a much darker interior room, with green wainscoting and ceiling, and dark, carved ma-hogany throughout. A large, green billiard table squat-ted in the dead center of the room.

At the front of the house, next, was a large room with a polished floor almost like a gymnasium. There was a huge mirror on one wall, with a ballet-style *barre* for practice. On the other side, a single bowling lane. There were no pins or balls anymore, but once again, Henry marveled at the party life and recreation available to the idle rich, once upon a time. *Mine now.* For a brief moment, he toyed with the idea of ordering a set of bowling pins, but there was no automatic setting device, and he didn't have the luxury of servants to reset the pins for him. Maybe he could reprogram a drone? He shook his head. A project for another day.

The doorway on the other side of the gymnasium led into the main ballroom again. On this side, before the entrance hall, was a small lobby and toilet. Henry took advantage of the toilet. The flush handle was up on a tank mounted high on the wall. He pulled it, and although the toilet did flush, the rattling and clatter of the pipes sounded like a steam train was crashing into the house. He peered closer at the pipes and mechanisms, just as something broke and shot streams of water into the room and all over him.

Soaking wet now and still shaking from his earlier scare, Henry fumbled around for the shutoff valve. There wasn't one down by the toilet but looked like something up nearer the ceiling. He stood on the toilet seat gingerly and reached up, turning off the unplanned shower.

Well, shit. He grumbled as he tried to flick water off his hands. He dripped his way out through the small lobby into the ballroom and around the corner to the entrance hall where most of his stuff was still piled high, waiting to be unpacked. He was digging out some dry clothes when he noticed something by the door that made him suck his breath in.

A large pile of ash sat in each corner. Again. Henry swept up the ash and dumped it outside—farther away, this time, on the edge of the woods.

Maybe I'm tracking it in somehow.

———————————

Got to relax. Deep breath.

Henry had made a pot of tea—literally in a cooking pot—and was sipping it from a thick ceramic mug in the upstairs parlour. He was going to settle in the master bedroom's corner turret but had found this large, octagonal room at the other end of the balcony. The balcony clung close to the walls high above the grand ballroom below, wrapping around from the grand staircase on one end to the parlour and attic stairs on the other. There was another entrance to the front toilet from the parlour, shared with the master bedroom.

He sipped the tea again, enjoying that he had brewed it from raw, loose tea leaves, not one of those horrible electronic laser cartridges. But he grumbled at the mug. *Not exactly Victorian elegance, now, is it?*

Still, it would do. He leaned back in the large, overstuffed chair. He'd put one of his towels on it as a defense against spiders and mouse turds. Henry sipped at his tea and looked out over the landscape.

Naked fingers of trees grasped at the dull gray sky. Hills rolled into each other and occasionally broke off, forming an often jagged landscape. Ridge after ridge, receding into the clouds and fog in the distance.

Hard to tell where fog ends and clouds begin. He took another sip.

This part is perfect, he thought, watching the approach. From here, smack in the middle of the front of the house, he could keep an eye on the approach up the driveway. There was only one way up the mountain. If he had to, he could post a drone to watch the entrance.

He sat there sipping his tea for a long while. Once Henry felt relaxed and restored again, he decided to take a quick look at the basement, if only to evaluate whatever other plumbing problems he might have to deal with.

The entrance to the basement was from the servants' staircase, which Henry thought made sense as it was sandwiched between the grand ballroom and the kitchen. *Easy for staff to fetch supplies.*

He gave the heavy, oak-and-iron-strap door a hearty tug, but it reluctantly opened only a little, moaning with each degree of arc. He braced his shoulder and wedged the door open enough for him to get through. The stairs down to the basement were long and steep—and surprisingly narrow—leading down beyond sight into a dark abyss. He flicked the light switch at the head of the stairs. Nothing. He flicked it again, rocking it up and down. Still nothing.

"Of course," he sighed and went back to his pile of stuff in the front hallway to get an LED panel.

Henry climbed down the steep staircase carefully, LED in hand. Each step creaked louder than the last, a rising cacophony echoing through the endless darkness.

New plan. First find the electrical service panel.

Very few of the lights in the house seemed to work; at the very least, he'd need to replace a lot of lightbulbs. *Can't live life with an LED in hand all the time.* He reached the bottom at last—it seemed more than a one-story climb—and looked back up the staircase. *Door seems so far away from down here.*

This part of the house was in even worse repair. It smelled funny, like rotting dirt. Not the rich, healthy dirt smell of the greenhouse, more like the smell of decay and death—of things returning to the dirt. Along the walls of the staircase, the paint was peeling in large, curled sheets. Even parts of the plaster walls themselves were crumbling away, exposing the wooden lath behind.

Like skin off a dying man. He shuddered at the macabre thought and started down a large, central hall-way.

And then nearly slipped in a puddle of water.

Swell, another leak, he fretted. It wasn't fresh or clean water, either. It had a reddish-brown look to it. *Rust?* He looked up at the ceiling carefully and at the adjacent walls. There were no pipes here. No sign of water anywhere else.

Now just where the hell did that come from? Henry sighed. He clearly had a lot to learn about plumbing. But first things first. On to the electrical panel. He swept the LED up and around.

The ceiling was high and vaulted, with archways made of bricks. A long, central hallway running the length of the house disappeared into the gloom. Openings on either side were filled with darkness, spilling out into the hall.

Storerooms? Henry wondered. *More like a maze.* He shone a light down one of the openings and saw what looked like more openings off to each side.

He decided to stick to the main hallway, still looking for the electrical service. Down the length of the house he went, finally seeing the old black metal of the electrical panel on the farthest wall. Cables going into the panel looked very organic, more like vines. Henry looked closer and realized the electrical wires were covered in some kind of knit fabric. *Oh, that looks safe.*

Henry opened the door to the panel, which made a horrible, metal-on-metal screech, like some wild animal caught in a trap. He forced the little door open fully and shone the light inside.

Fuses? For fuck's sake, Henry moaned as he surveyed the panel. No circuit breakers or intelligent sensors. Just little bits of metal in twisty glass holders. He'd read about such things but had never seen any in real life. He flicked the LED around, and mercifully there was a faded, crumbled paper box with extra fuses in it setting on top of the crumbling masonry where the panel was cut in. The writing on the fuse box itself was dim, faded pencil. He squinted but thought he could make out the word "BASEMENT."

He unscrewed that fuse and looked at it closely under the light. It was blackened, smoky looking. *That's got to be bad.* He took a fresh fuse from the box and replaced it. Back down the long, dark hallway, up the narrow and claustrophobic stairs, he flicked the light switch, expecting to see a warm suffusion of light fill the basement.

What he heard instead was a scream.

A screaming, shrieking shower of sparks exploded from the light fixture near the head of the stairs and repeated at intervals, popping right down the spine of the basement. The spittle of fire flared suddenly, then sputtered out quickly, leaving only a rolling echo of the crackle of misguided electricity.

Henry stood silently, stunned.

Frosting, Henry thought as he mindlessly licked the spoon. *A perfect snack. No pretension; it knows its place. Not supposed to be the main attraction, yet everyone knows it really is.*

He was sitting in the kitchen, licking his wounds over this latest defeat. *Fuck. I can't even get the lights on.* The whole house was out now. He had a couple of LED disks for light, but they wouldn't last more than a few days without recharging. He jammed the spoon down into the can of frosting and came back with another heavy load.

What the fuck am I going to do?

The electrical, the plumbing, the… the what?

The feeling. That feeling.

Something wasn't right. Henry had had the shit scared out of him how many times now? But there was nothing to be afraid of. There was no one here. He was alone, alone with the decrepit mansion that needed more repair than he was capable of.

Shit. Shit fuck. Damn.

Henry stared vacantly at the rear wall of the kitchen.

It was then that he noticed something: That wall looked different from the rest of the kitchen—and from the rest of the house. Everywhere else he had seen was plaster and lath construction, rich upholstered wall coverings, detailed wooden carvings, that sort of thing.

But not here.

No, this wall was much more plain. It looked like simple plywood or recently manufactured "builder's board," made from God-knows-what. Featureless, simple striations. It was out of place in a house where every surface was sumptuous, detailed, and exquisite.

Why is the kitchen wall different?

He cleaned off the spoon, reveling in the pure delight of the chocolate frosting. Kitchen, power, plumbing. The trio kept repeating. Kitchen, power, plumbing.

I've got to go clear my head. Henry headed out the front door.

Henry figured he could use the long driveway to take walks. It was maybe a half-mile down from the house to the gates, double that from the gates down to the main road. He could walk from the house down to the gates and back; a nice quiet stroll, alone on the packed gravel, as the sun slid under the horizon.

Crunch crunch crunch. The sound of his feet was all he could hear. That, and the quiet rustling of the leaves as the wind went by. Every now and then a large bird—a hawk, maybe, or a turkey vulture—would fly overhead. It was so quiet along the road that Henry could hear the beat of the bird's wings as it pushed itself along and aloft.

He shook his head in wonder and appreciation.

He'd *never* been any place in his life that was so quiet, so peaceful. This kind of environment just didn't exist in the megapolis. It was incredible, the sense of solitude, peace, and absolute aloneness. No one knew he was here, no one could track him down, ping him, trace him, nothing. Just Henry and the wild wind. *This* was why he wanted the house. He'd figure out the mechanical problems somehow. This was worth it. Free, safe, alone.

But as he was smiling inside at this very private thought, he heard something else—another set of footsteps, just after his own. Clear and distinct. Not an animal or leaves. Footsteps.

He stopped in a heartbeat and whipped around, looking up the driveway back toward the house. There was nothing, no one there. Henry wrinkled his face in confusion and jerked his head back the other way, looking again down the path, ahead toward the gates. Nothing there either.

Henry stood there in the quiet for a moment, hearing nothing but the wind rattling the last few straggling, crinkled leaves clinging to the trees. Cautiously, he took another few steps and then stopped and listened.

Nothing.

He walked again with a stronger, determined stride for a few moments before stopping suddenly and listening carefully.

Again, nothing.

Silence like he'd never known in the megapolis. Silence that denied any activity or movement. Any life at all. Nothingness.

He shook his head again. Must have been his imagination. An echo, or something, of his own footsteps. He made it down to the gate without incident and leaned with his back against the patient and unmoving wrought iron. He didn't feel like going all the way down to the main road, so he decided to head back up to the house before it got too dark.

Henry listened carefully the whole way for footsteps that weren't there.

Five

Henry camped out in the master bedroom for his first night in the house. The feather-stuffed bed was ancient, and maybe usable, but it would need a good airing out and maybe a beating. Henry tried, but he couldn't budge it, not by himself. He'd brought a sleeping bag, figuring there might be a problem, and stretched it on top of the high mattress facing the windows.

It was already darker outside than he'd ever experienced. A growing, impenetrable dark of night, hiding the whole world in its shadows.

He had one of the LED panels for light, for now, at least. Henry had noticed that Rudder's had bulk candles; power outages were probably not unheard of out here. He made a mental note to pick some up tomorrow. Better to not rely completely on the LED panels. Always have a backup.

It was cold in the house. Whatever combination of electricity and plumbing it took to make the heat work, wasn't. The sleeping bag was rated for outdoor weather in this climate band, though, so Henry wasn't too concerned. He hunkered in and zipped it up. The LED was set to dim slowly, Henry liked to drift off to sleep that way.

It was nearly fully dark outside, the dark of absolute nothingness. There was only the faintest hint of light from the LED. Despite the insulated sleeping bag, the cold of the house reached in and grabbed him anyway. He shivered, rolled over, and tried to get comfortable. But it was hard; not only was he colder than he was used to, but the confines of the sleeping bag also made it almost impossible to spread out into a reasonable sleeping position. He felt like he was stuffed in a giant sock. Which, he realized, wasn't far from the truth.

He was almost asleep, rolling back to the side he had just come from one last time, when he thought he saw something through half-opened eyes. A shadow, large and bulky, moved against the far wall. Sliding, gliding along the wall—not walking.

He jerked up, tried to sit fully upright, but the sleeping bag restricted him. He only made it about halfway up, eyes snapping wide open. There was nothing there.

Fuck, fuck, fuck, he chanted as he wrestled with the sleeping bag that engulfed him and managed to get his torso out. He slapped the LED to full brightness and realized his chest was pounding, breaths tumbling along in sloppy bursts. He looked all around the room in a frantic explosion of tangled limbs, trying to get out of the sleeping bag altogether. He did but not before crashing to the hard wooden floor in an angry and cursing pile.

"Double fuckweasel!!" he yelled aloud. Only then, awkwardly arrayed on the floor, did he stop thrashing about and instead listened carefully. Nothing. No footsteps, no doors slamming. Silence. The heavy, crushing silence of the deep wilderness at night. All he could hear was his own heart, slamming into his chest wall.

He leaned back against the feather bed. *What the fucking hell was that?* The drapes were open. He had cracked one of the windows open a little to try and get some fresh air, figuring it was better to breathe the outside air, cold as it was, instead of the musty and moldering air that had been trapped unwillingly in the house for who knows how long. Henry got up, disentangling himself from the sleeping bag and bedclothes completely, and walked over to the window. He looked out over the nightscape.

The moon had come out by now, bright and shining through the naked trees and casting grotesque shadows on the ground. *Like bony hands, scrabbling against the hard earth…* Henry tried to put the thought out of his mind. *Stop it. You're just freaking yourself out. It was just a shadow—a tree branch, or a passing bird or bat or something.* He reached up and drew the heavy drapes closed. Whatever it was, he didn't need to have the living shit scared out of him again tonight.

He stretched the sleeping bag out on the mattress again, smoothed it, and climbed back in again. *Sure would be nice to get some sleep.* He tried once again to try and find a comfortable configuration.

Gusts of wind slapped the house hard enough to make it creak and groan. Henry had rolled onto his side and was almost asleep when he heard a rattle. A rattle that sounded just like someone trying the doorknob. He jerked, stiffened, fully awake and listening.

Nothing.

Just the wind.

Exhaustion took him, as Henry hadn't gotten any sleep the night before, thanks to the long drive up here. But then, in that dim and murky place between the shores of consciousness and nightmare, a scream pierced the night—right in Henry's ear.

And not just any scream—a bone-chilling, bone-shattering, bloody scream of frantic terror and pain. Henry had left one side of the sleeping bag unzipped, and his hand shot out to hit the LED but missed and knocked it off the nightstand entirely. He bent forward, stretching out of the sleeping bag to try and reach it, and fell once again off the bed and onto the floor.

"Mother of all fuckers!" His hand shot out, into something warm and wet in the dark. "Sweet jesus! Fuck! Fuck!" He slammed hard against the bedframe as he reflexively jerked backward. He was fast running out of swear words. With his left hand, he groped frantically in terror to find the fallen LED panel. He swatted it, and it quickly filled the room with its pale, insufficient light.

The room was empty, quiet.

There was no one there. Nothing there. The door was still shut, the drapes still pulled. He was alone.

Henry lay crumpled and curled in a ball on the floor.

Dawn arrived, red-rimmed and swollen on the horizon. Henry felt the same. He sat in the cold kitchen for a while with a mostly tepid cup of tea, waiting for the library in town to open. Esmeralda had said he could come in today and work a bit, helping to reshelve books, catalog a few new items, all the sorts of things that needed doing. Henry figured he could use some company, and a break from the house for a few hours might be a good idea.

He rubbed his temples. *What the hell happened last night?* He wasn't usually prone to nightmares. Seeing shadows, hearing screams… his imagination was working overtime.

Dad would have called me a coward. A 'fraidy cat. Scared of the dark. Scared of a few noises. It's wild forest. Of course, there will be animal noises.

The shadow was probably just a large bird on a bright moonlit night. The scream? Maybe an owl. Branches rubbing together. A wolf in the woods. *Sure, that's it,* Henry convinced himself. He'd read about that once—wolves in the woods could sound like little girls screaming. *Oh, wait, or was that coyotes?* He frowned. He'd check at the library.

Henry got up from the kitchen and walked through the grand ballroom, through the billiards room, to the breakfast room, loud creaks announcing his every foot-step. The growing light of day filled the southern end of the house with light, and he felt better for it. He'd need to get a little table and chair for this room, set it near the French doors out to the patio. He shook his head, trying to clear out the shadows from the previous night.

You let yourself get freaked out, he chided himself. In the morning light, the house was once again magnificent, quiet, peaceful. Henry reconsidered going to the library—he didn't really need a break from the house, but he did need to do a little research on electrical and plumbing systems.

And wolves.

A violent thunderstorm came up out of nowhere and drenched the house and landscape just as Henry was leaving for the library. He was mopping himself off while describing his evening's experience.

"Coyotes. Not wolves," Esmeralda said. "Especially up on that ridge. Probably a den of coyotes in the rock face. Nothing to worry about, especially." But then, with a sudden look of concern, she asked, "You don't have cats, do you?"

"No." Henry smiled. "No cats, no dog—no pets at all. Not yet, at least."

Esmeralda nodded with relief. "Very good. Not really the best environment for pets up that way. Too many woods and wild creatures."

"Speaking of wild creatures, do you have a lot of albino deer up here? Pure white?"

"Not that I'm aware of." Esmeralda shook her head. "Why do you ask?"

"I almost ran into one on the drive up, and there's an image of a white deer on the floor at Weatherly. Made me think maybe they were common?" Henry asked.

"Well," Esmeralda pursed her lips, "in the time of King Arthur and his knights, a pure white deer was a sign that it was time to pursue a quest. In Celtic myth, in general, a white deer was seen as a message from the otherworld."

"I don't think I'm in any position to take on a quest at the moment," Henry admitted as he added to a growing pile of children's books from the cart.

"How do you mean?"

Henry absently straightened the pile. A copy of the very popular *Together We Win: Civics and Puppies!* was on top, its garish cover featuring an adorable dog with unnaturally large eyes holding what looked like the scales of justice. Henry wondered when children's books jumped that shark. He dismissed the thought and answered Esmeralda.

"I fried the electric service somehow. You should have seen it, sparks everywhere. Like an old-time fireworks show."

"Well, I'm sure that can be fixed—" Esmeralda began.

"And then I took a shower."

"Sounds perfectly normal—"

"From the water closet in the toilet," Henry said. "Now there's no water either."

"Oh. I see." Esmeralda was quiet for a moment. "I know you said you wanted to work on the house yourself, and I admire that, but perhaps you might think about getting some help in upfront, to jumpstart things a bit? Get off on the right foot?"

Henry grabbed another couple of books off the cart, including *You're Okay!* featuring a pathetic-looking child sitting alone on a megahighway. *The hell's that all about?* he wondered but added the book to the pile anyway.

"It sort of galls me to throw in the towel after *one night*," he said, biting off those last words like stale bread. He shuffled a few innocuous books featuring shiny, cartoon-style hyperloop cars. "But I think you're right. Just to help get things started in the right direction. Maybe. But I don't know anyone in town yet. I wouldn't even begin to know where to ask."

"Oh, pish," Esmeralda said, expelling a gust of air. "That's no worry. I've lived in this town my whole life. I know everyone, knew their parents, and probably met their grandparents in my youth. Paul and Enrico. That's who you need. Brothers. One's an electrician and network tech, the other does plumbing and structural repairs. Enrico's wife is a fantastic cook, by the way; if you're offered a meal of any sort, take them up on it. You won't regret it."

Henry looked up from the books he was sorting by age group, astonished. "Wow. Seriously? That's great. How do I get in touch with them?"

"I'll message them right now," Esmeralda offered. "You going back up to Weatherly after we're done here?"

"Yeah, that was my plan. Might stop off at Rudder's for some candles and things."

Esmeralda made a face. "Candles, maybe. I wouldn't buy his produce on a dare. His idea of 'fresh' vegetables is... overly optimistic."

Henry grinned. "I sort of got that impression already, thanks."

She made a series of gestures on her mobile, and a few moments later, a soft chime prompted her to smile. "You're all set. The brothers will be up this afternoon."

"Thank you so much for that," Henry said. "I really appreciate it. Seems to be getting colder; some heat would be great!"

Esmeralda smiled gently. "Of course, no problem at all. After we get these books from the children's reading circle reshelved, I have another treat for you."

Henry raised his eyebrows. "What's that?"

"Have you ever seen a card catalog?"

Bang. The noise echoed from the front door through Weatherly Hall's empty ballroom like a guitar box.

Bang. Bang.

It took Henry a second to realize someone was knocking on the door.

With a damn pipe wrench. Then he realized it might actually be so. He opened the front door to the two brothers, Paul and Enrico. Neither appeared to be holding a pipe wrench or anything else large, but one seemed to have especially large hands.

"Are you J?" the one with normal hands asked.

"Yes, that's me," said Henry after the briefest pause, remembering to use his alias. "You must be the brothers Esmeralda recommended? Thanks so much for coming out today."

"Paul," said Normal Hands.

"Enrico," said Big Hands. "Whadda we got here, J?"

His accent was strange. A mix of several dialects Henry couldn't quite identify. Old Bronx, a little Mex-american, maybe some—

"A big mess, I bet," Paul chimed in.

"Pablo!" Enrico hushed him, gesturing floridly. "Let the man speak."

"No, it's okay," Henry reassured them both. "He's right. Paul, is it? Yes, it's pretty much a mess. Place has been abandoned for at least fifteen years, according to the broker. I tried to replace a fuse, and the whole basement lit up like a sparkler."

"Sparkler?" Enrico gave a look. "You sure go for the old-fashioned things, doncha?"

"I suppose so." Henry grinned, suddenly very self-aware. "I took the job of overseeing this house, so yeah, there's that." He thought it a good time to reinforce his cover story.

Paul wrinkled his face. "Fifteen years? Probably more like thirty." He didn't elaborate.

They all stood for an awkward second before Henry offered, "Ah, okay. Well, come on in, let me show you what we're up against."

Henry led Paul and Enrico through the front door— noting the once-more fresh piles of ash or soot in the corners. If the creaks from Henry's footsteps were loud, the creaks from three full-sized adults were downright cacophonous. Echoing groans surrounded them as they moved through the ballroom and around to the servants' staircase and basement door. "Power's completely out, so there's no light down there. Panel is at that end of the house. There's leaky pipes somewhere. The toilet on this floor doesn't work…" He trailed off.

Paul stepped in. "What do you want us to look at first?"

Henry thought a minute, then told them, "House electricity first, then heat, then at least one toilet. Then we can talk about the rest."

"Okay, we'll see what we can do," Enrico said, lighting up an LED on his belt. The two descended into the dark of the basement. Henry thought a moment but did not join them. He headed to the kitchen instead. *Might as well have some frosting before it goes bad.* He realized that was a stupid argument to have frosting for a mid-afternoon snack. The house was as cold as a refrigerator anyway.

Leaving the kitchen, he wound his way through the house back around to the study at the front of the house on the north end, on the other side of the kitchen. An ornate, curved, and carved desk and matching chair was still here and some wonderful built-in bookcases in the walls. He sat at the desk and stared idly out the big window facing the front of the house, licking a frosting-laden spoon every so often.

"Mr. J? Mr. J?" a voice echoed through the boomy ballroom.

"In here!" Henry called out. "Front of the house."

Enrico popped his head in, followed by the rest of him, holding what might have been a dead snake. Or a thick vine. It was a little bit fuzzy, dark brownish, with blackened bits at the end that could have been metallic once.

"What the hell is that?" Henry asked.

"This is a big part of your problem," Enrico replied. "This is part of one of the main power cables coming into the basement and feeding the panel."

"Power cable? It looks like a jungle vine!" Henry exclaimed.

"I know, right?" Enrico nodded vigorously. "Fabric insulation, not polymer. I saw this hairy-looking stuff and I said, 'Man, this looks like something right out of Gilligan's Island!' "

"Gilligan?" Henry asked. He didn't understand the reference.

"One of the first television comedies. Mid-twentieth century. Man, you should brush up on your classics!" Henry made a face but Enrico continued, waving the antique wiring. "Anyway, yeah, this wire is so old… I can't even make jokes about it. It's just ridiculous, man."

"But you can fix it, right?" Henry asked, concern growing in his voice.

"Well, no, not fix, really. Replace. But the whole house is filled with this and worse. Some of the rooms upstairs aren't even wired for electricity at all; there are gas lines and lamps. Have you even tried any of those?"

Henry shook his head and Enrico continued. "To replace *all* the wiring… man, that's a huge project. *Huge.* I'd need helpers and it would take, oh, I don't know. Weeks? Months, maybe? I mean *huge*," he repeated, waving his hands wider and wider.

Henry sighed; he had sort of expected as much, especially after the shower of sparks in the basement. "Okay. Well, long-term, sure, we can talk about that, but what can you get working today? Nothing fancy—no intelligent sensors or anything, just circuit breakers or even fuses."

Enrico turned the burned wire over in his hands thoughtfully. "No, can't do fuses; they don't even make those anymore, man. Old stock only, and that's not even legal. So we'll need a new panel, at least. I can get power to that with fresh cables and *maybe* over to the boiler late today or midday tomorrow."

"And then?" Henry asked hopefully.

"And then whatever you want, my friend." Enrico shrugged. "We can go room by room, section by section, fix up whatever you need. Outlets, lights, switches."

"Okay," Henry replied. "Heat, then lights along that main hall in the basement first, then power to the kitchen, and we'll go from there. It's a big house; it doesn't have to all be fixed at once."

"You got it, boss," Enrico said and left the study through a small lobby out to the main ballroom, creaks following him. Henry heard him on his mobile, already ordering supplies. More creaks meant Paul was headed this way. Paul passed him in the ballroom and came in.

"Ah, here you guys are," he said.

"How's the plumbing? Is it all wrecked, too?" Henry asked, dejection plain in his voice.

"Oh, no, not at all. Well, not mostly," Paul said. For brothers, he sounded nothing at all like Enrico. Enrico had a more distinctive accent, and words tumbled in a frantic rush to get out. Sometimes he skipped a few in his enthusiasm. Paul was more measured, maybe more polished, somehow?

"Nice thing about plumbing," Paul continued. "The main pipes themselves can last for hundreds of years. They found some pipes down in Old Manhattan that were that old, before it sank, of course. No, the pipes are fine; it's the fixtures you've got a problem with."

Henry leaned back in the chair and asked simply, "Oh? Do I have to replace everything, like with the electrical?"

"No," Paul shook his head. "Not that bad. The boiler is a little sketchy but mostly in working shape. I think it's only twenty or thirty years old, not too bad. Fuel line is gunked up, but I should be able to get that cleaned out and working by tomorrow. For the baths and toilets, well, you're lucky the house doesn't have a whole lot of those."

"Yeah. Two on this floor and two up on the bedroom floor, that I've found. I haven't been up to the attic yet; that should mostly be servants' quarters," Henry said. "If you could get the bath and toilet working off the master bedroom upstairs, and then this one here next to the study, that would be great for starters."

"Sure thing, no problem," Paul replied cheerfully. "There are some leaking spots in the basement but they don't seem too serious. I'll know better once we get some better light down there."

"Fantastic," Henry said. "Don't let me keep you."

"I'm on it!" Paul waved and headed off to their truck for parts and tools.

Henry felt an immense wave of relief wash over him. Premature, perhaps, but at least he had knowledgeable help on the case. Some of the hope crept back in, cautiously, carefully, but it was there.

Maybe this will all work out after all.

Six

Earl Rudder was a scrawny man, made of tightly knotted rope under leathery skin and few words.

"What are you going to do about it?" A large woman, apparently a disgruntled customer, was building up a full head of steam aimed at Earl.

Earl shrugged. "Nothing. You opened it already."

"I'll send my husband over, and he'll give you a piece of his mind, Earl!"

"I couldn't possibly take the last piece," Earl retorted.

"Wha… why, you, you… well, I never!" the woman blustered.

"I'm sure you don't," Earl flung the classic barb and turned his back on the woman, who flounced out the door leaving wisps of steam behind her.

Earl's helper, a young, blank-looking boy, rolled his eyes at his boss's approach to customer service.

"Keep rolling your eyes, kid. Maybe you'll find a brain back there," Earl snapped. "Is there some reason you didn't finish unloading those crates?"

The kid hurried to the back of store, maybe to address the crates, maybe just to get out of the danger zone.

Henry smirked to himself. Not really the sort of exchanges he was used to back in the megapolis. Oh, people surely harbored such thoughts but rarely dared speak them aloud.

He found two kinds of actual, old-fashioned paraffin candles with wicks. Long tapers and squat, utilitarian-looking cylinders. He grabbed several of each and wandered toward the back of the store to look for the old stock fuses he'd seen. In what had to be the dingiest corner of the store, he found a few dusty boxes of glass electrical fuses. He grabbed those as well and headed up to pay.

Earl wordlessly scanned the items himself. Slowly.

So manual up here.

"I'm working up at the old Weatherly place," Henry offered, trying to make conversation.

"That so?" Earl wasted no effort on any additional commentary.

"Yeah, it's a pretty wild old place. Don't suppose you know anything about it, heard any stories or anything?" Henry kicked himself almost as soon as he said it.

Oh, Lord. Seriously? Hi, I'm new in town; is my house haunted? That's what it was going to sound like. Henry bit his lip.

Earl actually looked up as he finished scanning. "Don't be scared of the dead, son. Be afraid of the living."

———————

Henry walked down the driveway toward the gate. It was late, and the familiar dull, lifeless gray settled over the landscape as the day drained of color and life. Silence came with it. There was nothing to be heard except for a barking dog, very quiet, very far away.

It had been flurrying on and off all day, and the clouds seemed to finally make up their minds and commit to starting an actual snowstorm—early, the first of the season. The flurries intensified as Henry walked, swirling around him as the wind hurried to and fro.

He was going to pick up a package delivery from AmazeMart. Henry was only now appreciating the necessity of the modern supply chain. He could order almost anything legal, from anywhere in the world, and have it delivered here in the middle of nowhere—often within a day, rarely more than a few days.

Orders for merchandise "came from corporate," of course. There was nothing anyone could trace that showed that Henry ever ordered anything at all. He used the burner phone more than he'd planned to, along with a set of deeply nested VPNs, so anyone with abnormal curiosity would just see corporate orders delivered to a corporate holding.

Nothing to see here…

Rudders was okay for candles and vintage fuses, which were no longer commonly available, and it helped his cover to buy food and sundries there. But the selection was necessarily limited.

Too limited, Henry grumbled to himself.

He really wanted to live locally, off the grid, and not be dependent on globalism. But, he had to admit, that attitude would only get you so far. Tools, food, entertainment—Rudders just didn't cut it. So here he was, trundling down the driveway to pick up yet another bundle of necessities.

The house faded behind him into whiteout as the snowfall quickened. The small cardboard boxes were right there, predictably just outside the gate where drones had dropped them off.

How did the world ever work without drone delivery?

He opened the gate, dragged the boxes up the driveway a bit, and closed the gate behind him, snow filling the air around him. Henry picked up the boxes and headed up to the house.

Up ahead of him on the road, he saw the outline of a person. A man. Just for a moment, a shadow of a figure in the snow.

What the…?

Henry blinked, and there was nothing. Just snow, gently falling at first and now pinging against the trees as it slowly changed to sleet and freezing rain. He sped up, trying to get up to the point in the drive where he thought he saw someone. There was still no one there. No footprints.

He shook his head.

Must have just been a trick. Optical illusion. Just the wind and the snow.

As he was thinking this, he heard something rustling in the woods off to his right. Something large was moving through the brush.

It was probably just a deer, or a dog, or something.

Henry ran the rest of the way.

There's a special silence to new-fallen snow. The world, with all of its sorrows and pain, is quieted. The blanket of even a light snow dampens the hustle and bustle of animals in the woods, people on the streets, even birds in the air. All becomes still; quiet.

Henry was in the dining room, looking out the grand windows to the fields beyond. Floodlights from the back of the house lit up the gently falling snow. Only a few centimeters had accumulated so far, but it was enough to bathe the known world in quiet white.

This really is a fantastic property. Henry sipped a rare red wine that he'd ordered from an Old French estate. France hadn't existed as a country for quite a while now, but the old vineyards had survived the latest political upheaval and likely would survive the next as well.

That's the real secret, isn't it? Just keep moving. Survive. Ignore the latest regime and whatever nonsense they bring into the world. Just keep moving.

In the unearthly quiet, Henry heard some kind of howl out in the woods. It probably carried farther than usual in the quietude of the snowfall.

Always something out there with bigger teeth that wants dinner. That wants you *for dinner.* He shuddered.

The trick is just to... just...

Just *what?* Survive, sure. Keep moving? What other choice is there, really, other than curling up in a fetal position and withering away?

What is the trick?

He took a long swig of the velvety, rich red wine and appreciated its earth tones. Dark and hearty, not sweet. The brilliant hard white of snow against the dark black of the woods at night, the soft glow of the wine against the warmth of the house; Henry sighed. The lights flickered out briefly but came back on. Henry was getting used to that by now and tried to keep LEDs all around the house just in case. There was a growing pile of cardboard in the kitchen from a few deliveries and his moving boxes. Henry wondered if he could burn all that, somehow? Might need a carbon permit. Or maybe folks just buried trash up here. He'd have to find out. Yet another thing he never had to worry about back in the megapolis.

The house needed a lot of work, more than he'd thought and more than he could do himself. But that crippling realization had given way to a kind of relief— he didn't *have* to do it himself. Help was on the way. And it was a lot cheaper up here than it would have been in the megapolis. While there wasn't a lot of money left over, there was enough to hire some help. At least for a while.

Balancing solitude with practical necessities, with needing other people. *That's part of it.*

Maybe there is no secret.

Maybe there wasn't any single secret. Just a bunch of different secrets.

And you had to discover each secret by itself.

Seven

HENRY WAS UPSTAIRS IN THE PARLOUR, reading a book and watching Paul and Enrico go back and forth from their truck, arms laden with cables and tools. Henry was relieved to see the replacement cable actually looked like electrical wiring instead of the antique, cloth-covered primitive stuff that was in the house now. It was mid-morning, and they'd been working hard since yesterday. He could almost tell where they were in house just by listening to the floors creak as they passed.

He looked up from his book and saw Paul taking a break out by the truck, inhaling something from a pen-sized smoker. *Hey, I'm not one to judge. Whatever gets you through.*

Enrico called from the balcony. "Mr. J? You up here?"

"In the parlour," Henry turned and replied loudly. Enrico sauntered toward the front of the house along the balcony overlooking the main ballroom and up the several steps into the parlour. Henry heard him coming the whole way.

"You reading a real paper book? Man, you are *rocking* this whole antique vibe." Enrico spoke rapidly and grinned widely.

Henry gave a faint smile. "Yeah, well, I had lived in the megapolis all my life and worked in tech, so… kind of sick and tired of it all, you know? Good to get away from it all out here. That's why I took this job as caretaker."

Keep up the pretense, that's it.

"Hey, so I wanted to ask you something. It's just us in the house, right? No one else staying with you? Other workers, a lady friend maybe?"

At that, Henry frowned. "No, no one else. Just me, and you and your brother. Why do you ask?" He shifted in the overstuffed chair, suddenly uncomfortable. He could feel a tightening across his chest.

"Well, when I was down in the basement, I thought I… I mean maybe…"

There was an awkward pause. Enrico looked around nervously, waiting for the words to come. They didn't. "Oh, nothing. Never mind. It was nothing, man. Just an old house, right?" Enrico forced a weak smile and quickly changed the subject, talking faster than usual. "I just wanted to let you know the heat and hot water are up and running, and electric to some parts of the house. Oh, you'll need to schedule some synfuel delivery, man. Meantimes I've got to take my brother to another job, but I'll be back late this afternoon to try and get lights working in the basement."

Henry smiled. That at least was good news. "Great! I can't wait to try it out. Master bath is good to go?" He jerked a thumb to the room next door.

"You know it, boss!" Enrico confirmed and turned to leave.

Henry watched as Enrico went out front, and he and Paul took the truck and sped off down the driveway.

Wonder what freaked him out in the basement?

Henry watched the receding dust cloud of the truck disappear into the woods toward the gate. Dark thunderheads were forming, and the first low rumbles of thunder echoed in the distance. He frowned; thunderstorms were rare in the fall and winter in the megapolis. But they probably didn't have any weather control systems this far north.

Weatherly, all right.

He sat a moment, then realized it had now been several days since he'd last showered and was he feeling pretty grungy. He put a leather bookmark in the book and set it aside, stood up, and crossed the creaking floor of the parlour to a door that opened into the shared master bath. Henry went through to the bedroom itself and undressed, laying his dirty clothes on a corner of the big mattress.

Back to the bathroom, he flicked the light switch but nothing happened. *Bah. No power here yet.* But that was okay during the day. He left both doors open to let light in.

He eyed the large, footed bathtub. *Ah, screw the shower. A bath, that's the ticket.*

There was no touchpad or electronic controls for the tub, just some antique, oversized faucet handles. He gave one a twist but it stubbornly stayed where it was. With both hands, he gave a tug. The faucet reluctantly opened, and he felt the water grow warm.

Hey, hot water, for real. Awesome.

He sat on the toilet lid and waited for the tub to fill, testing the water temperature and adjusting it every few minutes.

Henry climbed in and settled into the hot water.

Ahhhhh. That's more like it.

He took a deep breath and relaxed into the warmth. Slowly, he could feel his muscles unwinding. It might take a lot of work—and a lot of help still—but the house would come together.

It will all work out. Just got to give it time.

He sat for a good while, until the bathwater started to cool off. Leisurely, he let the drain loose a bit to lower the water level. He turned the faucets to get a good mix of hot water, then leaned back and dunked his head underwater as the tub refilled.

That's when he heard it.

A long, low moan. Like a hopeless creature stuck in trap, dying. A moan of sorrow, loss, pain, and nearing death. Henry shot up out of the tub and jammed the faucets off, listening closely.

Nothing. As usual. No creaks, no footsteps—no indication anyone else was in the house.

He sat, listening to the intermittent drips from the faucet into the tub. Drip. Drip drip. Drip. They seemed to echo against the hard tile of the bathroom; other than that, the house was completely silent.

Cautiously, Henry turned the water back on and listened.

Still nothing. But he had a thought. Gingerly, he turned his head and put one ear under the water.

There was the moan.

He played with the hot water faucet, turned it down, turned it up, and could get the moan to go up and down in pitch. He turned the water off completely, and the sound left with it.

You asshole.

He shook his head, partly in frustration but also practically to shake water out of his right ear.

You stupid asshole, he continued to chide himself. *It was just the pipes.*

He grabbed the soap and actually bathed for a bit, then started to wash his hair, still grumbling to himself.

You keep imagining stupid shit, and you're going to go nuts. There's nothing wrong with this house. It's not haunted. There's no such thing as ghosts. It's just big and noisy, and you're not used to it.

He ducked his head under the water to rinse, when two loud *BANG* crashes plunged him into pitch darkness.

Fucking hell!

Henry practically exploded out of the bathtub, spraying water everywhere, and half slipped, half tripped to get over to the door. He could see light under the door as he fell against it, scrambling for the doorknob. It took a couple of frantic tries—his hands were wet, he was wet, the floor was wet, everything in the world was wet. The door opened, and he fell through into the master bedroom side.

Breathless and bruised, he rubbed the growing black and blue on his knee and realized what had happened.

Those assholes must have left a door open, and a stupid gust of wind caught the doors.

Wasn't the first time a door "mysteriously" slammed shut. *And won't be the last. Got to stop jumping like a damn...* He didn't know what. Furious, he grabbed a towel and started drying off and mopping up the swamp he had made.

Like a damn something that jumps every time it hears a noise. Fuck me. In the mirror, he saw bruises forming on his chest and forearms.

Fuck fuck fuck. Get it together.

After mopping up the mess, Henry figured he'd better go check the front door and make sure it was closed tight and that Enrico and Paul hadn't left anything else open. He came down the grand staircase, creaking gloriously, and checked the doors around the back of the house. Everything was tight and secure. He crossed through the ballroom back to the front entry way to check the front door.

Henry took hold of the doorknob and pulled. It didn't budge. The door was shut, firmly. *Well, that's weird. Maybe a window on the bedroom level or up in the attic?* He hadn't been up to explore the attic level yet. From the sketchy plans he'd seen, there wasn't anything but a maze of small servants' quarters up there.

Still, better take a look. He turned to head back to the stairs and noticed the corners by the front door.

A large pile of ash sat in each corner.

Henry crossed the balcony overlooking the grand ballroom and headed toward the parlour at the front of the house. On one side of the parlour was the master bath, on the other was a set of stairs he hadn't yet explored. He climbed the squeaky, narrow staircase to the dim gloom of the attic.

In a way, the attic mirrored the basement. There was a long, windowless, central hall running the length of the house, with small doors interrupting the blank and featureless wall. No silk or detailed carvings here, just peeling paint and crumbling plaster revealing the lath underneath.

He opened the first door, ducked, and went in. It was a small room, with a small window. There was no closet, dressing room, or storage of any kind that he could see. There *was* enough dust to stuff a mattress with, but no furniture. A glass globe with something like a ball of faded fabric in the middle hung on the wall, attached to a pipe that disappeared into the floor.

Ah, that must be a gas light.

The next two rooms were the same. The third bedroom was locked; an ornate brass keyplate seemed to indicate there was an ornate-brass key somewhere that would open it. Henry didn't have any extra keys, so that would be a project for another time.

Not much up here. Henry made his way down the hall. But there was a large room at the far end, clearly some sort of storeroom. It was packed full of broken furniture parts, cobwebs, paintings leaning up against the wall, the dressmaker's dummy that *every* old attic seemed to have, and a fair few things hidden under yellowed and cracked sheets. *Some other time.* Henry closed the door behind him.

All of the rooms had small windows, and all the windows seemed shut and sealed. No mysterious drafts from up here as near as he could tell. *Maybe the greenhouse door or something off the kitchen?*

"Hello? Hello? Mr. J?" Enrico's voice, thin and distant, drifted up the stairs.

"Be right down," Henry shouted, hoping Enrico could hear him. He headed back down the stairs, leaving the rest of the attic floor unexplored. He thought there should be another staircase and a few rooms above those—that's what it looked like on the elevation. But that was for another time.

"Hey, Enrico," Henry said as he descended the grand staircase.

"Hey, Mr. J. I brought more cabling and some utility fixtures, going to try and get some light in that basement of yours. Man, that is a big space. Have you seen all the little doors and siderooms and hallways and stuff, man?"

"Not in the dark, Enrico, no," Henry said with a good dose of sarcasm.

"Ha, that's a good one," Enrico laughed. "Good one, Mr. J. Okay, no problem, I'll go get started. I'm going to have to cut power to the whole house again, to work on the panel, so you'll be in the dark up here, too."

"I figured. No problem. I'll go read a book by the window."

Enrico headed through the ballroom back to the stairs, and Henry headed to the study at the front of the house. It was later in the afternoon by now, though, and the pale sun was at the back of the house, on the western side. He picked up his book and headed to the dining room, just past the servants' staircase.

The few dim, working lights went out with a *thunk* as Enrico cut the power. Henry pulled a chair over to the window and tried to get comfortable. There wasn't any furniture in the drawing room, so he had to make do with a hard wooden dining room chair.

Henry had barely gotten into the chapter where he'd left off when a horrific buzzing, crackling sound ripped through the house along with Enrico's high-pitched scream. The scream stopped first, abruptly, then the sizzle faded out. Henry jumped up and ran around the corner through the passageway to the basement stairs. He called down in the dark, "Enrico? Are you okay?"

Silence.

"Enrico? Enrico! Can you hear me? You okay, buddy?"

Nothing.

"Shit, shit shit," Henry muttered and ran around the corner the other way into the kitchen. There was an LED disk on the table. He grabbed it and headed down into the basement.

It smelled bad, an acrid smell of burnt flesh and wire. Henry waved his hands in front of his face to dispel the stink, but it just kept getting worse the farther he went. The weak light from the LED disk was not up to the task of the cavernous basement, but Henry kept to the main passage and headed straight to the electrical panel, hoping that's where Enrico was. And hoping Enrico would be okay.

Henry saw the stepladder first. It had fallen over, and its shiny metal legs stuck up uselessly in the air. Enrico lay a few feet away, face down on the damp floor.

"Enrico!" Henry shouted and fell on his knees next to the body. He rolled Enrico over, onto his back, and tried to check for a pulse or see if he was breathing.

Fuck, no, no, no. C'mon, man. Henry couldn't feel a pulse. He stuck his ear down next to Enrico's face to listen for his breath.

Just barely. Enrico was breathing but shallowly and not often enough. Henry had to get help, and there wasn't much time. He pulled Enrico's mobile out of his pocket. Dead. Couldn't even turn it on. Probably at least as fried as Enrico was.

Shitfuck. Henry dropped the phone and awkwardly tried to get underneath Enrico in a poor imitation of a fireman's carry. On wobbly legs, he half-straightened and charged down the passageway. He tripped on the first step going up the stairs and almost slammed Enrico into the wall. Breathing hard under the load, sweat rolling into his eyes, Henry finally made it to the top of the groaning, squeaking stairs.

For a second, he thought about digging out his emergency phone, but he headed through the ballroom out the front instead. *By the time they get here and roundtrip back to town… Oh, fucknuggets.* He barreled out the front door to his car, stretched Enrico out in the back seat, and flung the car down the drive toward the gate.

Out on the main road, he looked for his neighbor, Anahat, but he wasn't out in his garden. *For fuck's sake, the one time I need you…* Henry dismissed the thought and shot down the road into town to the urgent care office he'd seen near the library.

At least, that's where he thought it was.

———

"Mr. J?" the nurse asked. He was a slim fellow, with a pinched expression like he'd rather be somewhere else.

"Yes, that's me," Henry replied.

"Enrico is asking for you."

Henry sighed with relief. "So, he's okay then? He'll be okay?"

"The doctor will be in shortly," was all he said.

The nurse led Henry back past the reception desk through a large set of double doors and then into a patient room. Enrico was on the hospital bed, wearing the traditional drafty gown and stuck with more than a few tubes and silver wires.

"Enrico, you okay?" Henry asked as the nurse turned off to deal with other pressing matters.

"Oh, Mr. J., man, I feel like someone put my head in a vise. Then lit it."

"What happened?"

"Dunno. The power was off, man. To the whole house. Hand to God there was no juice coming into the panel. And then, like, it was all live."

Henry frowned. That didn't make any sense. He knew the power was cut—he'd seen all the lights upstairs go off at least. How could—

Just then the doctor came up, an older woman with dark brown hair put up in a long braid.

"Well, Enrico, welcome back. Haven't seen you for a few months."

"You two know each other?" Henry asked, startled.

Enrico squirmed. "Yes, well, stitches, you know. Best place in town to come for stitches."

"From what?" Henry asked and turned the face the doctor.

"Oh, no, not from me," she said. "Patient confidentiality. But, Enrico, do you consent to my discussing your current case with your employer?"

Enrico looked aside and waved his hand. "Sure."

The doctor faced Henry again. "Enrico was electrocuted. He's got pretty severe burns, and I'm frankly *shocked* that his heart is still pumping. No pun intended."

Henry blinked. Unusual to find a doctor with even a trace of a sense of humor.

"I'm not sure how that could have happened, Doc. I was there, and it sure looked to me like all the power to the house was cut."

"This happened in your house?" the doctor confirmed.

"Yes, ma'am," Henry replied.

"That's strange. Based on the severity of the injuries, I thought it must have involved a high-power transmission line or large industrial equipment. Not a residence."

"Well, it is Weatherly Hall. Not exactly a regular residence," Henry admitted.

The doctor blinked. "Even so, Enrico has sustained significant injuries. He's going to have a lengthy recovery time as we regenerate the burned tissues and such."

Enrico was softly humming, singing a song to himself, looking intently at the wall. It was then that Henry realized.

"He's doped up, isn't he, on some pain meds?"

"Of course," the doctor replied, with a look. "Some? Try 'all' of them."

Henry had to stifle a grin. She was unlike any doctor he'd ever met.

"Uh, I'm J, by the way," Henry said, extending his hand.

"Doctor Shelton. Fiona Shelton," she replied and shook his hand.

"I don't know how to contact his family—his brother Paul was out on a job somewhere, and his wife—ah, I don't remember his wife's name, I—"

"Not to worry, J," Fiona said, placing a hand on his shoulder. "We have his contact info, and it's been taken care of. You know, this sort of thing is our job here."

"Of course," Henry said, smiling, "Of course. You're all used to this. It's my first electrocution."

Fiona chuckled. "You get used to it. Electrocution, immolation, bar fights, ex-wife with a steak knife; we get it all."

"Wow. This must be the exciting end of town. I'm new here, really haven't seen any good bar fights or anything yet. Actually, I haven't even gone out at all yet." Henry blushed ever so slightly, swallowed hard, and in a completely uncharacteristic and impulsive moment, sputtered out, "I don't suppose I could ask to join me for a drink this evening?"

Fiona looked startled but recovered quickly. "What makes you assume I'm even single?"

Henry lost the blush and went straight to pale. "Ah… wishful thinking, maybe? Just looking for some conversation and good stories." His grin was weak and thin.

Fiona raised an eyebrow. "Well, I suppose that's better than assuming that being a doctor is automatically some sort of relationship repellent."

Henry laughed inside. *Oh, she's a sharp one, all right.* Out loud, he said, "Great then, say tonight around seven? I'm afraid the only bar I know is over by this dinky general store on the edge of town."

"You mean The Grumpy Yorkie?" Fiona asked.

"Uh, yeah, I think that's the one. Is that okay?" Henry was already second-guessing his choice of establishment.

"It's a dump," Fiona said flatly. "But it's also the only watering hole close by, so it will do. But let's make it 7:30; that will give me time to freshen up. You know, wash all the blood and entrails off and everything."

Henry grinned at that. "Certainly wash the entrails off, by all means."

Enrico rolled over, singing, "Entrails, entrails… Happy entrails, to you, until we meet again. Happy…"

Fiona rolled her eyes and turned to leave. "See you then."

Henry stood alone and watched her head down the hall to tend to some other horribly mangled or injured patient. *She is a piece of work, all right.* He shook his head and turned to say his goodbyes to Enrico.

"Hey, Enrico, I have to leave. But your brother is on his way. I think your wife, too. They'll be here soon. You take care, okay?"

Enrico stopped singing a moment and rolled his eyes around to face Henry.

"Mr. J!" Enrico said, as if seeing him for the first time, and sat up a little in bed. "The power was off, man. I'm telling you. The power. Was. Off. The house, man, hand to God that house tried to kill me."

Enrico sat back. "Tried to kill me, man. Tried to—" And then he nodded off to sleep.

Henry stood in stunned silence.

Eight

IN THE ICY SILENCE, the knock reverberated through the house. Henry had just gotten back from the hospital. The house was cold and dark—the power was still out after the accident. He was lighting a few of the candles he'd gotten from Rudder's to dispel the gloom when he heard the knock.

Henry thought maybe a few rugs would be in order at some point. Right now, the empty grand ballroom and most of the rooms on the first floor were just giant echo chambers, magnifying every little noise and floorboard creak.

Hell, half the strange noises I hear probably come from simple house creaking, mice running, pipes rattling, that sort of thing,

Henry crossed the grand ballroom and answered the front door.

"Hey, J," Paul said. "Okay if I come in?"

"Of course," Henry said, opening the door all the way and stepping back. "How's Enrico?"

Paul looked sideways. "Resting comfortable. Whacked out on meds still."

Henry breathed out, heavily. "Damn scary stuff. But I suppose he's used to it in his line of work, right? Probably not his first electrocution?"

"Actually, it is." Paul hung his head a bit. "He's gotten tickle charges before but nothing like this. He's a pro. Pros don't take chances. This sort of thing just doesn't happen." He spread his hands wide. "It just doesn't."

Henry frowned.

Paul continued, "Can I go down and check it out? Maybe get the power back on for you? No one has been there since the accident, right?"

"No, not a soul. I took Enrico straight to the urgent care, and I haven't gone down since I got back. But some lights and heat sure would be nice."

Paul smiled. "Sure. Enrico's the electrician, but I've helped him out enough I should be able to get you going again. Also, I want to try and see what happened."

"Be my guest." Henry waved toward the back of the house. Paul headed through the ballroom. Henry was going to the study to read in the fading daylight, then thought maybe he should go with Paul instead. "Hey, let me come down with you," he called across the expanse and jogged a bit to catch up. Paul turned and handed him an LED disk, and together they descended down the groaning, squeaking stairs into the persistent dark of the basement.

Not just dark, Henry thought as they left the staircase and headed down the long, dark center passageway. Their LED disks should have been bright enough, but they weren't. The expanse of the basement remained pale. Monochromatic. It was as if all the color had been drained from the damp rock walls and crumbling plaster.

They made it to the panel. Paul examined it for a few minutes, then pointed out the main disconnect to Henry. "Look. The disconnect is off. There should be no power to the house at all. No way Enrico could have been electrocuted in here. Where did you find him, exactly?"

Henry stepped back and walked over to the fallen ladder, at the end of a string of caged lights on the ceiling. He pointed. "Here." He didn't trust his voice to say any more than that.

Paul shook his head. "Doesn't make any sense. All right, well, let me test these circuits anyway. Maybe there's a second supply or something." He set the ladder upright and climbed up to where Enrico had been working on the wires. He grumbled after a few minutes.

"What is it?" Henry called up.

"It's nothing. Literally nothing. There's no juice up here, and there shouldn't be. Not with the power off. There's no way he could have..." He trailed off. "Okay, let's just fire it up and see what happens."

Paul went back over to the panel and threw the main disconnect back on. Henry heard the heat kick on, but the basement remained as dark as ever. "Enrico was working on the lights," he repeated.

"Yeah." Paul nodded and headed back to the ladder. "Let me see if I can figure out what's going on." He checked the wiring where Enrico was when he got electrocuted, then moved the ladder up and down the string of ceiling lights, back and forth to the panel, following wires on the walls and ceiling, testing, checking…

Henry watched him in silence for a bit, then started poking around the basement.

As he'd seen before, there were storerooms and workrooms off the main passageway, some of which led through to more rooms behind them, and even more rooms behind them. *Shit, this is a maze.* Henry ducked into an even smaller room. The walls were natural rock, whitewashed at some point. *More like graywash, now.*

This one had meat hooks on the wall, with a large grate feeding into a drain in the middle of the floor. *Must have used this to butcher game.* His stomach turned a little at the thought. He preferred synthetic or at least lab-grown meat, pristine in a little white shrink-wrapped tray at the store. Not hanging on the wall, blood draining into the floor. *Shudder.*

Most of the rooms were empty; it was hard to tell what they might have been used for. One had a large, person-sized slab in the middle of the room, with piles of bricks. Several small rooms had doors with handles on the outside only. *Damn, that's dangerous for a storeroom. No ventilation, no way to get out. Guess that's what happens when you don't have building codes or inspections.*

He wound his way back out into the main passageway. Paul was on the ladder, in a different spot, cursing under his breath.

"What'd you find?" Henry asked.

"Not sure," Paul admitted and wiped his eyes with the back of his hand. "I've got main power back on, and everything that Enrico worked on looks fine and seems to be working. There's no power to the basement lights, but it looks like there should be. Still no idea what happened to Enrico. If I didn't know better, I'd say it wasn't anything in the basement that electrocuted him. But you found him down here, right? It happened down here, not upstairs, and he wandered down here or—"

"No, no, nothing like that. I was upstairs; he was down here working, I heard him scream. He was here, all right."

"Well, Enrico is the expert. Everything looks okay to me, but what do I know? I flicked the breaker; you've got power back and heat, and lights where he'd fixed it already. More than that, we'll need him back."

"Yeah, okay. Thanks. No rush, tell him to get well first." Paul nodded and left the house just as it got dark.

Henry went upstairs to get ready to meet Dr. Shelton.

"McBurk!" The voice echoed down the hall, bouncing off the shiny, antiseptic metal surfaces, catching McBurk just as he tried to slip out the door. He sighed and turned to face his boss.

"Yessir?" He slurred the words together, not as careful to hide his disdain as he should have been.

The older man strode down the hall, anger mounting with each step. "Guess what I've been reading for the last hour?"

McBurk started to say something wiseass, then thought better of it. "I couldn't say, Lieutenant."

Lieutenant Tabor walked right up to McBurk, inches from his face. "I've been reading citizen complaints, McBurk. Quite a few of them. All naming you. A few of them actionable."

McBurk looked away but didn't relinquish any ground. "Sir, I—"

"Save it for the inquests. I can make most of these go away, one way or another." Tabor made a remarkably unpleasant face. "But not all. I don't know what you got away with back at Central, or who you pissed off to get sent out here, but I'm telling you right here and now, I will only go so far to protect you. If any of these citizen actions go through, you're on your own."

"Yes, Lieutenant. I understand," McBurk said in a tone that clearly said he may have understood but didn't care.

Tabor got even closer. "Let me make sure you do. You can go crack all the heads you want back in Central. I don't care. Those scum deserve it. But not here. These are my neighbors, my friends, my supporters whose money got me this position. You leave them the fuck alone, McBurk. Got it? Leave them the *fuck* alone!"

McBurk gazed up from his shoes, which he'd been studying closely, to look Tabor in the eye. "Yes, Lieutenant."

Tabor spun and walked back down the hallway, grumbling silently. McBurk thought he may have heard the word "turd."

McBurk relaxed and realized he'd been holding his breath. He turned, palmed the door control, and went into the locker to change out of his police armor and into civies. It wasn't the worst dressing-down he'd ever gotten, and he was pretty sure it wouldn't be his last, either.

McBurk had gone into police work dreaming of busting up drug rings, smuggling, prostitution—big crime. But none of that ever happened. It seemed all he managed to do was bust heads of low-level, petty scum.

Heads that needed busting. He unstrapped his weapons and sensors and hung them in his locker. Needed it, but still low-level. Never the big break, the big case, the big conspiracy.

He sat on the bench and sighed, holding his hand in his heads. *This isn't how this was supposed to turn out.* That one big case, the one he thought would make his career… but it didn't. He had violated procedure and got sent here to Newthington. *The ass end of New Yorkland.*

Drink. He needed to drink. A lot. On the outskirts. He knew just the place. McBurk tugged on his boots, reached into his locker, and reverently took out his leather jacket. It was real leather, from the 20th century, and had been his brother's, and his father's before that. They were both gone now, both killed in the line of duty.

He zipped up the jacket, feeling the weight of his ancestry on his shoulders, and headed out into the cold to The Grumpy Yorkie.

"Eric, bust any Girl Scouts or old ladies today?" Reginald asked as McBurk sat at the bar.

"Fuck off, Reg," McBurk barked.

Reginald sniggered. "What'll you have?"

"Usual," Eric McBurk muttered under his breath. Reginald nodded and poured him a double shot of Kentucky bourbon.

"How…?" McBurk started to ask a question and hesitated as he realized he might not like the answer. "How much is left?"

"Of the old stock, from old Kentucky itself?" Reginald asked.

McBurk nodded, solemnly.

"I can get maybe another two cases from my guy. After that, it's just whatever comes in from the New Confederacy."

"The new stuff sucks," McBurk grumbled and took a generous sip of the bourbon, letting it roll around his tongue and evaporate.

Reginald wiped the bar down with a cloth and nodded. "Yeah. Pre-war stuff is still the best. Maybe someday…" He trailed off and moved down the bar to wait on another customer.

McBurk played with the zipper on his coat. *Fuck, how did it all come down to this?* He took a larger sip of the bourbon. *Fuck it, enjoy it while I can.* He slammed his meaty fist on the bar top.

———————

Henry opened the door to The Grumpy Yorkie and was immediately surprised at how small the place was. And not especially clean. *God, what a dive.* But Fiona had said she'd meet him here and seemed okay with it. He took a table near the door.

The bartender came over after a few minutes. "Hallo, don't think I've seen you around before. New in town? Visiting?"

"Hi, name's J. Yeah, new. I was hired to take care of the Weatherly place," Henry said, a little more smoothly this time. The lie became easier on each retelling.

"Well, welcome aboard, Mr. J! My name's Reginald. Reginald Moore. This is my place." He gestured grandly. "What can I get for you this evening?"

"Ah, I'm meeting someone here," Henry stumbled a bit. "I'll just have a wine. Red. Something hearty."

"Got just the thing," Reginald said and whisked off to behind the bar.

Henry looked around. No more than a dozen folks spread around the space, most of which were just staring at the bottom of their drinks, hoping for some inspiration or revelation even though none came. One specimen caught his eye, a short, stocky man, built like a fireplug. Pink skin, balding, like something boiled. The man slammed his fist on the bar top, muttering into his drink. *Great, an angry drunk psychopath. Just what every bar needs.*

Reginald came back just then and delivered Henry his wine. Henry muttered his thanks but Reginald was already off.

The door opened, letting a flood of cold air into the room. Fiona strode in, spotted Henry, and walked over.

"Fiona!" Henry looked up and waved.

"J. So you found the place," Fiona said and sat down at his table.

"Wasn't so hard. Newthington isn't that big, especially here on the outskirts. What can I get you?"

Fiona had caught Reginald's eye, and he came over. "Oh, Reg knows."

"The usual, Doc?" Reginald asked.

"Sure, Reg." Fiona waved him off. "So, Weatherly Hall? That's quite the establishment. How did you find yourself here? You don't strike me as the 'outskirts' type."

Henry paused to gather his thoughts. He didn't want to be rude but didn't want to share too much, either. "Well, I had done a lot of IT work in the megapolis, and I guess I just wanted to, oh, I don't know. Try something different. Something real, you know?"

Fiona had set a steely gaze on Henry this whole time. Reginald came over and dropped off her Cosmopolitan. "Thanks, Reg," she said to his back and turned back to Henry. "So what do you think of Weatherly and Newthington so far? I mean, other than almost killing your electrician."

Henry took a sip of his wine and looked at the table. "Poor Enrico. He's going to be okay, isn't he?"

"Yeah, I think so," Fiona said. "Unofficially, of course." She took a swig of her cosmo and leaned in closer. "He thinks there's something going on at Weatherly. Could just be shock from the accident, of course. But you live there. Have you noticed anything… strange? Anything, er, unexplainable?"

Henry leaned back in his seat. "Well, no, not really," he lied. "I mean, it's a really old house. Drafty, doors slam when they shouldn't, can really creep you out on a cold dark night." He laughed bitterly.

She didn't.

He stowed the smile and turned more serious. "No, I haven't seen anything… unexplainable. Nothing like that. Just an old house. Rundown, dangerous in places. How about you? What brings a skilled doctor like you to a dump like this?" He smiled broadly again.

They kept talking.

———

McBurk leaned against the bar, scanning the room. Mostly the same old regulars. Except there was this new guy, sitting with that doctor from the urgent care place. Reginald swept back behind the bar, and McBurk turned around and motioned to him.

"Hey, Reg. Who's the newbie?" He jerked a thumb over to the table where Henry and Fiona sat.

"Fellow named J. Hired to take care of Weatherly Hall, I hear." Reginald deftly wiped a few glasses clean and stored them in one motion before moving down the bar again.

Weatherly Hall, huh? McBurk made a mental note to add Weatherly to the drone routes tomorrow. *Well, let's just see what he's up to.* He drained the last of his bourbon and stared across the room. He didn't like new people and decided he didn't like this new guy at all. Weatherly Hall had sat empty for a long time, long before he was sent here from the central megapolis district. Now this guy just showed up out of nowhere to fix it up? *Damn right that smells fishy.* He hauled his bulk up off of the bar stool and lumbered to the door.

———————

Henry swayed a bit as he fumbled the bulky keys into the lock at Weatherly. He wasn't exactly drunk, but that was more wine than he'd had in a long time. He and Fiona had talked all night long, until The Grumpy Yorkie closed. It wasn't love at first sight or any dreadful cliché like that. Just two lonely people who spent a few nice hours being less lonely.

He creaked the door open and listed a little to the left as he crossed the threshold. A large pile of ash sat in each corner. Again. Still. *Damn this house and its freaking dirt.* He wobbled across the empty ballroom and mounted the stairs to the bedroom.

Sleep came quickly but didn't linger. Henry couldn't get comfortable and kept waking up. He rolled to his left side, slept fitfully, then rolled onto his right. That wasn't working, so he turned back to his left, and came face to face with his wife, stone cold dead in bed next to him. Gray skin peeled back with bulging, swollen eyeballs. He leaped up from the bed and ran to his children's bedrooms. Their throats had been slit, beds soaked with their blood, dripping slowly onto the polished wood floors.

Drip.

Drip.

Drip.

Henry bolted upright in his bed, wet with sweat. Frantically, he jammed on the LED light. He was alone. Of course he was alone. He had no wife, no children. *What the fuck?* He swung his legs out of the bed and sat upright for a minute, trying to clear his head.

That wasn't me. Whose dream was that?

He got up out of bed and headed next door to the bathroom and filled a glass of water. *Water for hangovers. Fight dehydration.* The room spun a little—not a lot, just a little. He turned and heard a door slam in the hall. *Now what?* Henry tottered out the other door of the bathroom to the parlour and listened.

Silence.

He crossed the parlour and down the stairs to the east end of the balcony, stopping to listen across the great expanse to the ballroom below.

Slam.

Slam. Slam.

Three more doors slammed, one after the other.

Silence. No creaks, no squeaks, no footsteps.

Mother fuck! Henry scrambled across the parlour frantically trying to get back to the bedroom. He slammed the door behind him. Trembling, he sat upright in bed and waited for dawn.

Thin cold rays of morning slid through the window and poked Henry awake with a start. *Shit.* He grabbed at the bedclothes and pulled them close, shaking the cobwebs from his head. He was shivering. Some of that was from the cold.

"Okay, beer next time. No more cheap wine," Henry said aloud, hoping the sound of his voice would be a comfort. It wasn't. It just echoed slightly in the huge bedroom.

He got up and opened the curtains all the way, letting the pale sunlight flood the room as best it could. Birds flew past on their own urgent missions. Henry took a deep breath, relaxing in the serenity of it all, in the peaceful, natural world. The birds chirped their chirps, swooped and dived, doing all the things birds do on the edge of the forest.

Except for a pair of very large birds. Coming in on a straight line from the edge of the woods, straight for the house.

Henry jumped back into the room, away from the window.

Drones.

Nine

HENRY BACKED UP TO THE FAR WALL, as far away from the windows as he could. It was too late to close the drapes; the drones would have sensed the movement and possibly come in for a closer look.

But the drones didn't seem to alter course at all and just took a very unimaginative, simple circular route around the property.

Routine patrol scan. But that didn't stop his heart from racing. He cautiously went to the window again and watched as the drones came around from the other side of the house, returning the way they came down the long driveway.

Henry forced himself to take a deep breath.

It's okay. Routine scan. Large drones like these were almost always autonomous and not particularly nosy. Just out fishing for any easy evidence. Smaller drones, however, generally indicated serious trouble. Small drones meant an operator on the other end—and an agenda. One step away from a no-knock warrant and armed officers at the doors.

If they were really after me, they'd have sent the small ones.

Henry shuddered at the thought, still cold from the night.

I just have to avoid any facial tech.

Even though the drones had gone, for now, he closed the drapes anyway.

This complicated matters a little but wasn't entirely unexpected. Large drones he could keep an eye out for. Patrols were usually regular. They'd come right up the driveway next time, too. He noted the time.

Probably right about the same time.

Unimaginative. Big drones he could handle. But if they spotted something that begged closer investigation… He'd need counter measures.

I'll have to risk an order. He headed down to the kitchen to pull out the phone he'd hidden.

Henry entered the codes he'd memorized and quickly had a list of options scrolling on his screen. He picked the equipment he needed, including an extra hydrocell just in case, and paid via an anonymous crypto account, one of many he'd set up. Once the order was placed and he'd gotten the drop coordinates, he took the ID card out of the phone. Rummaging through the drawers of the kitchen, he found something that looked like a pair of pliers, only the hinge was at the far end. He turned it over a few times before he realized it was a nutcracker.

That'll do.

Henry stuck the ID card and a nail in the nutcracker and used it to smash the card. He left the pieces in the fireplace for good measure.

The drop would be there in a couple of days but in the meantime, he'd need to do some work down in the basement to get ready for the equipment. Before he could shore up the house defenses, he needed to fix the basement up with better light. And power.

Henry grabbed an LED panel—it was becoming a habit—and carefully climbed down the basement stairs. Funny that they seemed even more narrow than usual, and they weren't all that wide to begin with.

I'll bring light into this basement if it's the last thing I ever do. He immediately regretted his choice of words.

Best not be so dramatic.

He walked down the central hall of the basement, his LED panel casting shadows that glided up and down the uneven walls and empty openings as he passed, as if they were following him, circling and sneaking up behind him.

Of course the shadows are following me. It's how the light is angled. He tried to put the thought aside. Didn't make them any less creepy. Something about the way the shadows *glided* just wasn't right.

He got down to the end, and the ladder was still at the junction box. He climbed up, fresh bulb in one hand, LED panel in the other. Once up at the ceiling, he unscrewed the burnt remains of the dead bulb. It was no more than a charred husk—only the base remained, and a few shards of the casing.

That's no ordinary dead bulb. Henry frowned. How could such a powerful surge have even gotten to the house, let alone past the breakers? He figured that maybe the problem was in the bulb itself, a manufacturing defect that caused it to short out. Maybe the whole batch was that way, and that's why the whole string of lights went out at once. He hefted the bulb he had brought down from upstairs. This one had been working fine, so he was expecting it to work once he screwed it in here.

He was *not* expecting the sudden jolt as something slammed against the ladder, knocking it out from underneath him. The feeling of nothing but air didn't last long as the hard-packed basement floor slammed Henry hard, driving the breath out of his lungs first, then hitting his head with the full force of the fall. The LED panel had smashed and gone out, but Henry felt a different sort of darkness. His vision dimmed beyond mere black, and in a haze of blood-red pain, he blacked out.

Almost twenty hours had gone by, but Henry didn't know it. He woke with a start and opened his eyes but couldn't see anything. At first, he didn't know where he was. But the feel of damp earth and the smell of mortal decay reminded him he was in the basement. The pain made it clear he'd been injured.

His head pounded with a fierce ache. Gingerly, he felt his forehead and right temple, and discovered an unsettling combination of crispy dried blood and damp, sticky fresh blood.

Fuuuuuck.

Henry rolled over and sat up. He had no light, nothing on him that could make a light. Alone in the dark in the basement, with a growing fear that he wasn't actually alone. Something had run into that ladder and knocked him off. Something that was very likely still down here. He tried to breathe as quietly as he could and listen carefully but didn't hear anything special. No snarling, heavy breathing or scratching in the pitch black. Just silence.

And thank all the gods that may be listening for that.

Now on to the more immediate problem—how in the hell to get out of here? Slowly and gingerly, he drew his legs in and rose up to standing. He felt his arms and legs. Nothing hurt beyond what might have been a simple bruise, except for the apparent gash on his head.

Oh, Father would have loved this. Another dead end, another unique way to disappoint him. He always said I couldn't do anything right.

Henry reminded himself that his father was an ass and turned his attention to the more immediate. He turned slowly in a circle, peering through the impenetrable black for *any* glint or gleam that might help him orient himself. Very, *very* faintly he thought he saw an only-slightly-less dark area far in the distance. One slow step at a time, he headed for it, arms out stiffly and waving in front of him, hoping to avoid the harsh suddenness of a wall. Or anything more lively.

With each step, his stomach tightened a quarter-turn. His breath came a little quicker; the hairs on the back of his neck stood up higher. If he accidentally turned into one of those endless side corridors, he'd be as good as dead. No one was due at the house until Enrico was released from the hospital. That could be days, if not a week or two.

Henry stopped, his hands shaking. *Just keep feeling the way. There's nothing down here.* He tried to tell himself that, but he knew that was a lie. There *was* something down here. Maybe just some local wildlife—he remembered the squirrel that had scared the shit out of him in the greenhouse. But whatever was down here had to be a hell of a lot bigger than a squirrel to be able to knock the ladder over.

His left hand felt a wall, he hoped one of the side walls of the main corridor. He kept a hand touching it as he headed to the faint light that should be coming from the kitchen, down the staircase. It was a fine plan until his hand ran into something warm, wet and sticky, with a smooth polished center. Like a bone sticking out of human flesh.

"Jesus fuck!!" Henry screamed and jerked his hand back, the force knocking him off balance. He landed hard on his ass, still scrambling away from the wall.

He sat there on the floor, panting, weeping, and about to throw up, hugging his knees into his chest.

I can't do this. I can't live like this. Henry sobbed quietly, hoping not to attract anything.

Minutes passed, maybe even an hour. Somewhere in the back of his mind, he heard a distant echo, the snide snicker from his father. He could almost feel his bony finger pressing into Henry's chest for yet another lecture.

Yeah, fuck that. I'm better than that, and you know it.

Henry took a deep breath and stood up again, grimly determined. Hands in front of him only, step by slow step, he headed to the basement stairs.

In the kitchen, Henry found his small first-aid kit, rummaged through, and found a bandage about the right size for his forehead. He made a sandwich and coffeesynth, and noticed his hands were still shaking. Clammy. He took a bite, drank some hot coffee, and leaned back in the chair.

Food helped. He took a couple of deep, deliberate breaths and slowly began to feel like himself again.

Well, the basement is out. I'm not going down there again. Probably no one should go down there alone.

But he needed somewhere out of the way to install the drone countermeasures. If not the basement, then where? Henry clenched his fists, fingernails digging into his palms, and slammed the kitchen table as frustration welled up in him.

Damn stupid basement, squirrels trying to kill me, ancient wiring made out of tree vines. Not supposed to be this hard. He stood up quickly and slapped the odd-looking wall in the kitchen. *Stupid wall. Some half-assed repair job.* He slapped the wall in a couple of different places, but even if it were the result of some half-assed contractor, it remained solid and unyielding. A gust of wind made the house moan, which was always louder here in the kitchen for some reason.

"Fuck it. Fuck you, house," Henry said aloud and stormed out of the kitchen, through the house and out the front door, cursing at the two piles of reappearing ash on the way. "And fuck you, too!" Tears stung his eyes as he slammed the door behind him.

Out in the sunshine in the driveway, Henry raised his chin and screamed, "Arrrggh!!" at the top of his lungs, aimed nowhere in particular. Any gargoyles or statues that were watching kept their customary silence.

He stood there a long minute until his heart stopped pounding and his breathing eased into a less-ragged version of itself. He unclenched, beginning with his fists, and took a deep breath.

It was actually a beautiful day, he noticed. Clear blue skies, with a few thin clouds on the horizon, and the lazy late afternoon sun ambling down to the horizon. He shuffled around the driveway a moment, then walked around to the left side of the house, past the patio and then the greenhouse, down the hill slightly to a set of small outbuildings. He hadn't explored this part of the property before, and he really just wanted to get out and away from the house for a while.

Henry passed stone outlines in the ground, partial remains of the foundations of buildings lost to time. *Tool sheds? Outhouses? Animal barns?* No way to tell anymore. A larger building on his right was still standing, made of gray stone pillars and a mostly-intact roof. Large openings in the front suggested it had been a carriage barn, probably for horses originally, and cars later. He ducked in through a half-open, half-ruined door barely held up by iron hinges nearly rusted through. Single story, dirt floor, not much to see. It was dim inside and smelled of earth. But of good earth, the soil that's full of life and growth. Henry frowned slightly; this place had a very different feel than that of the basement of the main house.

He shook his head and wandered back out into the daylight.

Dirt is dirt.

Down the hill a bit was a slightly smaller, more intact building, half set into the hillside itself. *Ice house, maybe?* Henry remembered reading that in the days before electricity, people had used blocks of ice from the winter to store food. The door was intact and swung open easily. Inside was a wooden floor, made of surprisingly wide planks of wood, worn from a hundred years of use.

Henry walked deeper into the shadows away from the door and saw an even darker rectangle along the back of the floor. As he got closer, he realized it was an opening— a narrow set of stairs leading down under the floor. He descended the creaky wooden stairs slowly, peering into the darkness underneath, lit only by a few thin threads of light that slipped between the floorboards. Again, the smell of damp earth here was healthier somehow; wholesome.

He walked around on the dirt floor but had to hunch a little as the ceiling wasn't quite tall enough for him. *This might work. There's no power out here, but there's room to install the anti-drone stuff.* He came back up the stairs and looked out the door of the shed back up to the house. *Line of sight. Perfect.* Now if he could just figure out how to get power out to here. He had planned to use the hydrocell to supplement the house power and buffer him from the frequent power outages. But it would work out here and have the advantage of putting the tech completely off the grid.

Henry continued walking down the hill, mulling over his options. A few more small sheds tilted this way and that, in various states of disrepair, but none as promising as the ice house. *If that's really what it was used for. That's what I'll call it, anyway.*

He continued down past the outbuildings, over the crest of a small hill. There, under a grove of ancient trees, was the family graveyard. Henry sucked his breath in.

"Shiiit," Henry hissed through his teeth. Surely there was no such thing as ghosts. Whatever was after him in the basement was just a wild animal or something—something explainable. There were no ghosts or dead bodies in the basement.

But here, this was an actual graveyard. With actual dead bodies.

Slowly, he walked up to the opening in the low, delicate iron fencing. Dead weeds and tall grasses choked out any kind of path or walkway and obscured many of the headstones themselves. But he could make out the names on the larger headstones near the entrance.

Morris. Mr. and Mrs., present and accounted for.

Henry waded through the crunch of dead grass and leaves toward the back of the small plot.

Fergusons. He looked around, brushed some tall, brown grass out of the way. *Lot of Fergusons.*

Back up the middle there was a small stone bench under a large sweeping tree, beautifully carved with florid swirls and comforting cherubs. Henry parted the grass, walked over, and sat for a moment.

So peaceful and calm here, not creepy or angsty at all.

He took a moment to look around more carefully. The fading winter sun had warmed the stone enough that Henry noticed. Even the breeze—usually a harsh constant at Weatherly—was gentle and not as biting today. Henry relaxed into the bench a little, ran his hand over the fine moss, and gazed up at the cool, crystal blue sky.

Henry realized this was most relaxed he'd felt in a long while.

In a graveyard, no less. Go figure.

Maybe it was his imagination, but somehow, he felt the souls here were truly at peace. Beyond the cares of this world. Nothing left undone, no cruel wrongs to avenge. Maybe that's why the house felt… different. Not at peace. Angry. He shook his head.

I'm sitting in a graveyard, of course, I'd think the house was…

He stopped short of verbalizing the word he desperately wanted to avoid.

Haunted.

The weeds in the graveyard inspired Henry, so he went back to the house and started to clean up the weeds that had encroached on the patios. He'd never used a hydrogen-powered weeder before, and it took him a few tries to get the hang of it. But before long, he was cutting through tall banks of dry flowing weeds that were trying to infiltrate the house.

Henry worked his way around the patio outside the breakfast room and back toward the greenhouse, clearing the grasping fingers of nature as he went. But, exposed outside of the house, he kept a watchful eye on the road. The drones shouldn't come on their routine patrol until later, but he couldn't rely on that. Not until he got the counter measures installed.

More and more thick, choked weeds fell to the weeder, and more and more of the glowing glass of the greenhouse saw sunlight again for the first time in recent memory. Henry had been at this a while, and as he kept an eye on the road, he kept an eye on his watch as well. It was getting close to drone time, and he was surprisingly hot and sweaty from exertion.

Good time to head inside, wash up.

The drones came and went, right on schedule. Henry missed it; he was well and safely in the interior of the house, bathing before going out. He'd decided that sitting alone in the house at dusk was a bad idea, and thought he might head over to The Grumpy Yorkie. He half considered pinging Fiona but chickened out.

Out of the house, yes. Ready for company? Not just yet.

The car eased down the driveway, slipping surely away from the house and down the road. There, in the dwindling twilight, he spotted his neighbor, picking away at the dry dead stalks of his garden, silent footsteps in the still of encroaching night.

"Anah! What are you doing out here this late?" Henry lowered the car window and asked as he pulled up alongside the garden.

Anah looked up at him and smiled serenely. "Ah, there's always something that needs your attention, isn't that right, Mr. J? I'll be here until my work is done."

"I suppose," Henry admitted. They made small talk for a few minutes, then Henry mustered enough courage to ask a bold question.

"I've… I mean, I think I've…" He hesitated. There was a pause.

"Yes? Go on, please," Anah prompted him.

"It's just… I don't know, sometimes I think the house at Weatherly is… out to get me. Mad at me, maybe. It's stupid, I know…" He shook his head, embarrassed that he'd even brought it up.

"Why is that stupid?" Anah asked, with perfect patience. "You had some, ah, experiences there, I imagine?"

Henry looked past him to the thick hedge that hid Anah's house. "You could say that. I mean, every house has its character, I suppose, and it's an older house with plenty of explainable mechanical problems. Leaks, drafts, that sort of thing." Henry found himself talking faster and faster.

"But it's not *just* that. It feels… I don't know, personal. Like the house wants to hurt me. It sure hurt Enrico pretty bad. His brother Paul said he'd never seen anything like it, and they are both professionals, but he'd never been electrocuted before, not like that, and then there's basement, and the ash, and…"

Henry trailed off, realized he'd been talking a mile a minute.

Anah just smiled and said, "I do not think you are crazy. But I think you are asking the wrong person. I do not know what you saw, or what you felt, or what you experienced. But if you want to know the house, to know the character of the house, you should know its history. Everything in this world is the way it is because it got that way, Mr. J."

Henry looked back at him, his face a mixture of puzzlement and regard.

Anah repeated, "However it is now, it got that way. You should find out how." He turned and walked back up the tilled rows toward hedge and house, silently moving through the gardens.

Henry raised the window, frowned, and continued on to The Grumpy Yorkie.

What a fucking dump, Henry thought, and not for the first time as he nursed a beer at the bar. The bars and restaurants in the metro were shiny, clean, with art-work and clever lighting. Not here. Dim flickering bulbs, maybe even old-fashioned fluorescent tubes, bathed the customers in a ghastly and unflattering glow. The floor didn't bother trying to look like hardwood, or marble, or tile, just battle-scarred plywood or builder's board.

But no one seemed to mind. And even Henry had to admit the beer was delightfully cold. He took a sip, almost alone at his end of the bar, but somehow, even with just maybe a dozen other folks, it was better than drinking by himself.

He'd gotten near the bottom and was considering ordering another when a hefty, fireplug-shaped man sat down heavily next to him.

Oh, great, it's the pink-skinned psychopath.

"You're new here, aren't you?" the fireplug man pro-claimed. It wasn't a question.

Henry hesitated, trying to figure how to best play this. Short seemed best. "Yes. Name's J." He bowed, city-style, but the man stuck out his hand. Reluctantly, Henry extended his hand as well. Handshakes were decidedly out of favor since the rash of post-war pandemics.

The man grunted, a thoroughly unpleasant sound, seized J's hand and tried to crush it. J stifled a grimace and squeezed as hard as he could. After a few tense seconds of such arrogant posturing, the man let go.

"J, huh? Not much of a name. What's the rest of it?"

"My friends just call me J," Henry replied and took a last swig of beer.

The man narrowed his eyes, displeasure clearly written across his pink. boiled face. "You're up at Weatherly, aren't you? Hired as caretaker or something?"

Oh, he's not suspicious of me at all, is he? Henry thought sarcastically.

"Something like that, yes." Henry remained non-committal.

"So, who owns the property now?" Fireplug-man tried to appear less interested and nodded to Reg to refill his glass.

"Not really sure," Henry lied. "I was hired through a temp agency at first, then they made a permanent offer, but it's through some kind of holding company in Central. So, some kind of conglomerate, I guess." He shrugged as if he didn't really care. But instantly his mind drifted off.

He had bought the estate through not just one but a whole series of shell companies. Steward and Associates, which was owned by Escape Partners LTD, which was owned by Holiday Investments Inc, and then a couple of others, all in different jurisdictions and mostly going through countries that weren't part of the Nine Eyes. It would be *very* hard for anyone to trace him as the owner. Very hard to find Henry Jamal Steward.

Fireplug, meanwhile, was close to glowering. "Well, we'll just see what I can find out at the office, then." A pause. "I'm the law in this town, Mr. J. Did you know that?" He tried to burn a hole in Henry with his eyes alone.

Henry glanced back at him, trying hard to appear disinterested. "Whatever. A paycheck's a paycheck. I've got a job, and I like the place." He slapped a few tokens on the bar and got up to leave. "Nice to meet you, Mr.?"

Fireplug stood up slowly and dramatically to try and reach his full height, which wasn't in any way impressive. "McBurk. *Officer* McBurk."

"Yes. Well, have a good evening then." Henry turned and left.

McBurk watched him silently, burning with obvious dislike.

Henry headed out into the cold of the evening.

Shit, shit, shit. That little prick is going to be steering drones out as soon as he can, and I'm not ready yet. Good thing he was off duty or he would have gotten a facial scan already. Can't have that.

He got in his car and squealed out of the parking lot a little more quickly than he meant to.

It should be there by now. I'll have to go pick up the dead drop tomorrow. Can't wait anymore.

It was a race now, and it might be a close one.

Ten

IT WASN'T YET DAWN as Henry sped along the outer fringe of the Wastelands. Lightning lit up the sky behind him, followed by long, slow rolls of thunder. But at least he seemed to be driving out of it.

He was off the main road already, on what charitably could still be called a road. Past a series of small, decayed buildings, like a row of missing teeth, he turned onto what was little more than a path across a vacant field. As he crested a small hill, he saw the half-torn-down remains of several small shacks and decrepit buildings.

That must be it.

He double-checked the GPS coordinates using a modified, privacy-shielded receiver. He'd picked that up at the first drop, a simple and relatively safe affair located under a park bench back in the megapolis.

This pickup, however, was something different entirely. An illegal GPS receiver was a minor thing, maybe a small fine or a few days in jail. But the anti-drone tech would get you shot on sight.

Henry stopped the car, pulled on the prosthetic face mask in case it was a trap, and waited a minute before getting out.

Oh, I'm not any kind of super spy, or raging activist, or stealthy hacker. Well, maybe a little of that last. Just a little.

Henry thought about his job working for the government—nothing special, just a low-level grunt doing low-level paperwork.

Such an antique word. No one has actually used paper for work in decades. Language idioms die hard.

He worked with petabyte storage devices, taken fresh off the most sensitive drone operations. Too sensitive to transmit over even the most heavily-quantum-encrypted net, these data wafers were carried *by hand* from whatever hot zone they came from into his data center and processed locally.

It may have sounded exciting, but it really wasn't. In reality, it was almost exclusively boring as dirt, unless you happened upon an analysis that you shouldn't have. He'd heard rumors, just gossip really, about some co-workers who maybe saw something they shouldn't have. At least, that was the word going around after they disappeared. But no one knew for certain.

Despite that, working for the state did give one a certain measure of protection that the common man didn't have, and that was worth a lot in the years after the war. Enough for Henry to put up with a lot from the new regime, for a long time.

But then he got lucky. He made a bundle of money on unregulated cryptocurrencies at just the right time, and it was the opportunity he'd been waiting for. He'd quit his job but paid in advance for his apartment for a full year. Even if they had the slightest reason to come looking for him, the trail would be stone cold dead. All electronic traces and "paperwork" would still show him back in Central for most of a year after he'd physically left.

Unless, of course, he got nailed by a drone scan.

Yeah, not going to let that happen. Not by some low-level local prick.

Henry opened the car door slowly and stood by the car for another minute, just watching and listening. Nothing. He was alone, as near as he could tell.

He turned on a separate device, a short-range ultrasonic transceiver. Keyed in the codephrase from the transaction, and some listening bit of tech replied with a directional signal. Henry lined up the device to one of the shacks. It was important to pick the right one, which you could only do if you had the right codephrase. The other buildings in this cluster could contain explosive booby traps—it helped to keep out the curious, or thieves trying to nick the drop. Henry approached the building as indicated.

It was a shack, made mostly of cement cinderblock and corrugated metal. The front door was half off its rusted hinges. He pushed his way through. The main room was mostly empty, just some rubble on the floor from a half-caved-in roof. Pre-war graffiti on the walls demanded that someone "go back where they came from" and "speak good american." Henry snorted. Stupid, ignorant, hateful people. Served them right. But at such a cost.

We won, at least. If this counts as winning.

He crossed the littered floor to a small bathroom with a toilet and sink. He lifted the distorted, dirty mirror over the sink and underneath was a modern, glowing keypad. He punched in the code for the drop, and the side wall of the bathroom clicked and slid back a bit. Henry went over and pushed the fake wall all the way, revealing a small store room. Filled with his gear.

Thank the gods.

Henry was relieved. Most of the time the dead drop market worked perfectly well, but there was always a chance you'd get ripped off, and any ability to complain was pretty limited. Oh, sellers were supposed to post cryptocurrency bonds in case of non-delivery, and there were blockchains to support their reputations, but it wasn't like you could go to the courts if you got cheated.

But it was all here: a few rolls of tight antenna mesh, a small, non-networked hydrocell for power, and a couple of processing racks. Being extra cautious, Henry went back outside first and scanned the horizon, now easing toward a dark gray. All remained quiet and solitary.

Just how I like it. He smiled.

He loaded the gear into his car, left the GPS and ultrasonic transceiver in the drop room, and took the small bag of dust and dirt by the door. After sealing the door shut again, he backed his way out of the building, scattering the dust over his footprints as he went. He chucked the now-empty bag into a pile of rubble and got out of there as quickly as he could. He had to get back and get everything set up before that psycho cop could get orders for a drone mission.

The sun was just peeking over the horizon when Henry made it back to Weatherly.

The ice house, or whatever it was, turned out to be perfect for Henry. He unrolled the wire and composite mesh flat onto the dirt floor under the outbuilding, hooked up the rack processors, and held his breath as he plugged in the powercell. The racks quietly powered up, and he began the initialization sequence. Four small drones launched from the racks and quickly found their way up the stairs and out into the yard.

Given the size of the house and surrounding area, Henry had programmed in a generous defensive perimeter. This would take a few hours. But when the initial scan was done, the gear would trick any incoming drones with a fake "background image" that would not show Henry or any other people on the property. Just the buildings and background, and even that could be edited to omit any incriminating points. It was actually a lot more complicated than that, as the AI would also compensate for time of day, season, local weather, and so on, at all visible wavelengths and infrared, but ultimately it would make Henry invisible to the drones, and that was what he needed.

He'd be safe from the scans, at least.

———————

McBurk frowned as he scrolled through endless listings of real estate transactions, ownership shares, foreign registrations, and more. He'd been at this for several hours now and was no closer to finding out who owned Weatherly Hall. That was pretty suspicious in itself.

"Someone went to a lot of trouble to make this hard," he muttered.

"Talking to yourself now, McBurk?" Lieutenant Tabor stood in the doorway, eyebrows raised.

"Yes, sir, some of the wittiest conversations I've ever had, in fact." McBurk's voice was dry, flat.

Tabor ignored McBurk's ego for the moment. "You are logging all data requests appropriately, with an audit trail, of course?"

"Yes, sir, but—"

Tabor had started to turn to go.

"—there's something strange here."

Tabor visibly sighed and turned back around. "What?" he asked with a bluntness that clearly telegraphed his desire to be anywhere else just now.

"Someone is fixing up old Weatherly Hall, up on the outskirts."

Tabor struggled for a moment to place it. "That ancient barn up on the hill? Might as well be in the Wastelands. Is it even in our jurisdiction?"

"Barely, sir. But it is. I ran into this guy who says he's been hired as a caretaker up there, by some corporation."

"And?" Tabor was really hoping this was going somewhere, and soon.

"Well, that's just it. That corporation doesn't really exist. It's a shell. Owned by another shell. I've been trying to trace the actual owner for hours, and I keep getting rerouted to dead ends. Someone has gone to a lot of trouble to hide the owner's identity."

Tabor frowned and took a step closer. "How much trouble, McBurk?"

McBurk swung the panel around. "Check out this trail of owner's shares and registrations—and look at the foreign ones."

Tabor whistled. "Wow. Looks like somebody needed a hobby. Or a girlfriend. Any way this could be legit? Result of a bunch of mergers, acquisitions, takeovers?"

McBurk shrugged. "Dunno. Maybe. I'm not an accountant. But it sure looks like someone's trying to hide something to me."

Tabor scrolled through the data feed a bit more, saw the dead ends in several uncooperative countries, and nodded. "Yeah. That doesn't look right. Patrols report anything?"

"I sent regular patrols over the last few days, but they didn't find anything—or anyone around. Nothing obvious." McBurk threw up his hands.

"Hmmm," Tabor hummed. "Alright, order and execute a detailed scan. It's probably nothing—just some big corporation's tax dodge, or a pre-war property vestige that's just getting shuffled around. You know, leftover paperwork."

"Or," McBurk insisted, "it could be someone setting up a drug lab, or organ trafficking, or—"

"Let's see what the scans find before speculating," Tabor warned. "And *especially* before bashing any heads in."

Tabor shook his finger at the panel. "If this really is a coverup for something criminal, we do it *legit*. By the rules. If the prosecutor loses a big case just because you were sloppy and gung-ho, well, I'll make sure he knows exactly who to take it out on. You got that?"

McBurk nodded solemnly but grinned wide as he could on the inside. He was confident that he'd find some kind of incriminating evidence from the drone scans.

Even if he had to plant it there himself.

Henry vomited into the sink, a gush of blood pouring out his throat. He tried to spit to clear his mouth, and realized those hard bits were his teeth. He jerked upright to look in the mirror over the sink when he saw that his left eyeball was missing. Nothing left but a ruined, empty socket. In fact, most of the left side of his face was gone. Blood was streaming from his face, filling his mouth. A violent, desperate scream rose from his bowels, but as he opened his mouth, he felt that he had no tongue. It was gone.

Fuuuuuuuck! Henry bolted upright in bed so hard that he slid off the side and fell to the floor in a tangle of sheet, cover, and sweat.

Just a nightmare. Just a nightmare. You're okay, he told himself, feeling his face and confirming his tongue was, in fact, still in his head.

He was walking around the balcony on the second floor, just walking, a single candle in his hand barely illuminating the floor in front of him. Circling the bedrooms, the entrance to the upper floors, the grand staircase, swirling down into the dark gloom of the first floor. The sun was rising, but no light penetrated the inky gloom below. Compelled by forces he didn't understand, Henry descended the stairs and came out on the balcony on the second floor, and continued walking. Circling the bedrooms, the entrance to the upper floors, the grand staircase, swirling down into the dark gloom of the first floor.

Wait, what?

His brain struggled. He looked up at the ceiling. He was on the balcony. Still on the balcony. But hadn't he just gone down the staircase? He shook his head. Had he been drinking? The sun was blazing through the windows in the parlour out onto the balcony. But not downstairs. And below that...

Hell.

Torture. Suffering beyond imagination.

His breath was coming in ragged clusters, panting, trying to catch himself. He could hear the grandfather clock in the entrance hall. Each tick echoed through the empty house like the peal of thunder.

Tick.

Tick.

Tick.

And then it stopped.

The sun went out.

Gasping, he sat upright in bed, the faintest rays of dawn grasping through the window to find him.

Just a nightmare. Just a nightmare, he told himself again. Only this time, he was actually awake. He hadn't fallen out of bed; he hadn't been walking around with a candle.

He slipped out of bed and padded to the bathroom. The faucet squealed reluctantly, as usual, but he got his drink of water. It was early dawn, and although Henry was hoping for a few more hours of sleep, that wasn't going to happen now.

Henry was miserable. He hadn't yet gotten a truly good night's sleep in this place, and his upper back and shoulders felt as knotted as a kid's macramé project. It was cold in the house in the morning, as it always was. He grabbed a soft hoodie and pulled it on.

Out of the bedroom, he wandered down the grand staircase, which led him to the first floor just as it should. He shuffled into the gymnasium room at the front of the house. He idly ran his fingers along the barre, watching himself in the large, wall-sized mirror.

Somebody's dance practice, once.

It had been years since he'd done any sort of yoga or stretching exercises, but Henry thought maybe that would help now. He felt in pretty rough shape and was trying to do too much at once. All the work loading and unloading the equipment and setting it up, all the work around the house...

Yeah, maybe some stretching out would help.

Standing in front of the mirror, he tried to ignore his bloodshot and bleary eyes and concentrated on loosening up his shoulders. He hunched them up to his ears, then down again, trying to remember the thing about breathing while stretching. He did this a few times and noticed that his shoulders weren't coming down evenly. With a frown, he hunched up just his right shoulder, but something was wrong.

The fabric of his hoodie pricked up over his right shoulder, like it was caught on something. Quickly, he lowered his shoulder and looked around. There was nothing behind him, nothing near him that he could see—either in the mirror or by looking around. Shaking his head, he moved on to his left shoulder.

Same thing. A weird lifting, puckering, like his hoodie was caught on something, or—

Suddenly, his hood flew up violently off his back and past his head, heaving toward the ceiling and lifting him off his feet. Frantically, he kicked and swatted at the empty air as the floor fell away from him, and then it just stopped. He smashed into the polished wood floor, his right side taking the brunt of the trauma.

Henry gurgled a *shit* or two and passed out.

"I'm saying I saw something down there. A woman." Enrico was adamant.

"Enrico, you were electrocuted. You could have seen angels and flying saucers just as easily." Dr. Shelton shook her head.

"No, ma'am, no, not during… like before. Before the accident. There was something in the basement. Some_one_, I'm telling you. But not really there, you know? But I saw her! Or it. Or something."

Dr. Shelton checked off a few boxes on the panel in her hand and made a few notes from the readouts on the monitors on the patient. "Enrico, are you telling me that the house is haunted? That you saw a ghost?"

Enrico turned his head aside, made a face. "Maybe. I don't know. There's no such thing as ghosts, right? But I'm telling you I saw something. And then *this* happened." He gestured to the hospital room.

Fiona shook her head again. "Enrico, you've had a traumatic experience. You are, frankly, lucky to be alive. You may have had damage to your memory, damage to your reflexes, who knows what. I'm not a neurologist. I don't know if you really saw something, or if your memory was affected by the accident. But I'm fairly positive there's no such things as ghosts."

Enrico looked back at her. "But you don't know for sure, do you? You can't prove that there aren't."

"Well, no, I suppose not. But put it this way. I've seen a lot of people die in the hospital, and not all of them quiet or peaceful. But I've never seen a ghost, or a spirit, or anything like that. And wouldn't you imagine that a hospital would be just *filled* with ghosts? Lots of folks die here. It'd be a natural. But I've never seen a ghost, and neither has anyone else here. None of the staff. None of the other doctors." She shrugged. "It just doesn't happen."

Enrico frowned and went quiet.

Dr. Shelton finished up on the panel in her hand. "But good news, you'll be going home. I've pinged Pamela; she'll come and pick you up tomorrow morning."

"Don't… don't tell my wife about what I saw," Enrico said. "It would frighten her."

"Your secret is safe with me, Enrico," Dr. Shelton said. "Now do try to be careful on your next job. In fact, you might want to wait a week or so before going back to work. Give your body a chance to rest up a bit more?"

"Sure. Thanks, Doc," Enrico said flatly.

Fiona left his room and continued her rounds.

God, I need a drink. Maybe if she made it down to The Grumpy Yorkie, she'd run into J.

She smiled unexpectedly.

Eleven

THE WHITE LIGHT WAS BLINDING. Henry blinked, blinked harder, but still couldn't form an image. He could hear words, but they were muffled, far away. He couldn't make out what they were saying. But it sounded important.

Smell came to him first—it smelled funny here, wherever *here* was. Like disinfectant. Alcohol. Maybe he was at the bar?

Words drifted by; he caught a few of them.

"…know where you are? J? Can you hear me? Do you know where you are?"

"No." Henry managed to croak the word through a burning and dry throat. "Water…"

"Not yet. J, do you know what day it is?"

Rarely. Every day is a weekend.

"No."

The white light shut off, replaced with a red-black glow from his overstimulated eyeballs, gradually revealing the thin, sickly greenish glow from industrial lights overhead.

"J, can you tell me who the President and Chief of Police of New Yorkland is?"

Henry cleared his throat, which was largely ineffective due to a lack of saliva. But he was coming around and answered groggily, "Some shitbag."

The doctor laughed out loud at that. "Well, there's one right. J, do you know who *I* am?"

The blurry round blob came into sharper focus, and Henry blinked away the remaining mental cobwebs.

"Fiona! I mean, Dr. Shelton."

Now it was the nurse's turn as he let out a low chuckle, which was quickly stifled as Dr. Shelton shot daggers at him with her eyes.

Henry tried to raise his hand, realized he couldn't. "What happened?"

Fiona shook her head. "We were hoping you could tell us. Enrico and Pamela found you in the house, crumpled on the floor in the gymnasium. It looks like you fell from a decent height, but there wasn't a ladder or a balcony or anything in that room. Maybe you fell in the ballroom and crawled over?"

"Maybe," Henry said, noncommittal. "Who's Pamela?"

"Enrico's wife. She thinks you and Enrico are being a bunch of babies about the house and need a woman's touch to keep you out of trouble and from doing stupid things."

Fiona waved at the cast on Henry's arm, the IV lines, and bandages. "This doesn't exactly help your defense any."

"I suppose not," Henry admitted. And that much he felt was true—the house was more than he could manage, haunted or no, especially with a newly broken arm.

"My insurance, did you—" Henry sat up a little, and fought a rising panic that the urgent care staff had done a facial scan, or fingerprint/vein scan to identify him.

"Oh, no problem. I looked up your Weatherly Hall employer and got the billing authorization. It went through okay. Here's the confirmation, if you're worried." Fiona punched up a document and showed Henry the screen. It listed him as "J," not by his real name.

Henry lay back and tried not to look panicked. He took a deep breath and quickly changed the topic. "Shit," he said and looked down at his arm, encased in some ceramic composite. "What the hell am I going to do now? We're headed into deep winter, and the house isn't quite functional yet."

"You'll need some help, I suppose." Fiona made a few notes on her panel, waving the nurse on to the next patient. She leaned in close to Henry and whispered, "Listen, I want to talk to you about Weatherly but not here." Then she stood up and strode off.

Henry leaned back a little and stared at the nondescript, institutional ceiling.

Shit.

McBurk frowned at the screen. The drones had finished the next-level detailed scan, according to protocol. But the reports showed nothing of interest. Heat signatures showed a reasonable profile for a large, probably drafty house. No extra energy output, no visitor traffic—in fact, no traffic of any kind.

What the hell? Does this guy never leave the premises? Or is he even there at all?

Maybe the whole Weatherly angle was an excuse—a false lead. Maybe this guy J was holed up somewhere else. McBurk scanned the local feed for any other tidbits, any anomalies that might tie in. Nothing seemed out of the ordinary. Usual amount of drug and disorderly issues, some petty theft, domestic disturbances.

Always the same scum, McBurk gritted his teeth. He searched for any updates that contained the name "J" or "Jay." A new message popped up: *Subject named 'J' admitted to Urgent Care Facility #309.*

That's gotta be him. Well, that explains where he's at. McBurk grumbled. He wouldn't be able to look at his medical record directly without further authorization and attention, but he could go in through the insurance reporting.

Insurance code: 5403

McBurk looked it up, some kind of house construction accident. He drummed his fingers on the desk. He'd have to wait until J was back at the house before he could catch him doing anything.

And McBurk hated waiting.

———————

Paul was driving, Henry sat in the passenger seat with his arm and cast propped up. As they rounded the driveway, the creepy weeping statues threw long shadows on the gravel from the setting sun. Enrico continued to make his case, as he'd been doing for the whole drive from urgent care.

"Look, man, you need help. You hired me, you hired my brother here, and well, we're here to help you!" Enrico urged. "And my wife, my Pamela, she comes along too. She's a fantastic cook. Best cook ever. Hand to God."

Henry glanced over at Pamela. She was a little younger than the brothers, with very fine and long black hair, and a slim but possibly powerful build. She seemed the type to get stuff done. Maybe Enrico was right. But Henry was already feeling useless.

"I'm fine, Enrico, really," Henry protested as Enrico and Paul helped him out of the car.

"Of course," Paul chimed in. "But we need to finish up the work at Weatherly, and maybe that would be a little easier if we *all* stayed here for a few days at least."

"One extra on the payroll. I'll feed you all, and we'll get this whole project wrapped up and be out of your hair, Mr. J," Pamela said with confidence.

"Absolute-a-ly!" Enrico bubbled. "Everything will go better with Pamela here."

Paul shot him a look.

"And you too, bro, of course. J, we'll get you all buttoned up. No more hospital trips, though, okay?"

Enrico helped Henry through the front door of Weatherly, past the piles of ash in the front hallway, Paul and Pamela following behind.

"This is a terrible idea, staying in this deathtrap of an antique. At night," Paul whispered to Pamela. Pamela saw the dark expression on his face, punched him in the shoulder, and gave him a glare.

"Mmmmpph," Paul let out a stifled yell.

Pamela closed the door behind them, sealing them inside Weatherly Hall.

"Okay, try it now." Paul was lying on the floor, wrench and pliers in hand, underneath the small, antique gas stove.

Pamela turned the knob to let the gas flow and used a small laser lighter to ignite it. The ring lit up with a steady blue flame. "Yeah, babe, we're cooking with gas now!" she chortled.

Enrico groaned at the kitchen table. "Oh, honey, that was terrible. My ears."

Paul scrambled up from the floor. "You good now?" he asked Pamela.

"Yeah, I'll get dinner started. You guys go patch a wall or trap a vicious attack squirrel or something." She giggled at that last bit.

Enrico did not. "Hey, don't make fun."

Paul chimed in. "Seriously, stick to the kitchen and these rooms at the front of the house—everyone. Don't go off alone until we figure out what's going on."

"Nothing's 'going on' except that it's an old house that needs repairs." Pamela rolled her eyes at them.

Paul made a face. "Come on, Enrico, help me with some plastering in the hallway."

Enrico got up from the table and left with Paul. Henry stayed behind, resting his cast on the table as Pamela busied about.

"What are you making?" a bored Henry asked idly.

"You'll see!" Pamela said as she expertly chopped vegetables.

"Pretty handy with that knife," Henry commented.

"Been cooking since I could walk, I think. My mom taught me. I've worked as a cook, a chef, had a street cart once, you name it. I love to cook." She deftly flipped some sort of sauté in the pan without needing a spatula.

A quiet roll of thunder echoed off the hills. Pamela continued, starting a sauce. It smelled fantastic, and Henry realized he hadn't had a decent meal since landing in the hospital. Jell-O didn't count.

Hammer blows echoed through the house every now and then as Enrico and Paul set to work, and the occasional buzz of a saw. Henry had a book in front of him but just wasn't in the mood. He could turn pages one-handed, but it felt weird. And he felt useless.

A vicious crack of thunder hit so close that Henry was sure half the house had been flattened. The lights flickered once and went out completely. It was pitch black in the windowless kitchen, save for the faint blue glow of the gas burners on the stove.

"Well, shit." Henry sighed.

"No prob, Mr. J. Gas stove. I'm good." Pamela kept going.

Enrico and Paul were coming, Henry could hear the creaking floors as they approached, and the faint glow of their LEDs getting brighter.

"Man, you see that rain outside?" Enrico jerked a thumb in a vague direction outside the kitchen.

"Not from in here," Henry grumbled.

"It's like a high-pressure hose. Good thing we're staying here tonight, wouldn't want to go out in that. How's dinner coming along, babe?" Enrico asked Pamela and gave her a squeeze.

"Couple of minutes, all set. Find us some plates?"

Enrico and Paul set the LEDs down on the kitchen table, casting strange shadows around the kitchen as they set up for dinner. Henry moved his book off the table, feeling even more useless.

The house groaned as lightning cracked nearby, the rumble of thunder now nearly continuous. The rain was loud enough that they could hear it even in the kitchen, and the wind screamed like a wounded animal in a trap. They ate in silence as the storm raged, the light from the LEDs shone on their chins, casting deep shadows up over their eyes and making everything look creepy.

"This is delicious," Henry said in between bites.

"I told you, man! Best cook anywhere!" Enrico beamed at his wife.

Something screamed in the distance, and they all fell silent again.

"Um." Henry cleared his throat. "I think that's a coyote. In the woods."

"Sure," Paul said, but none of them were. Silence grew long again like a shadow itself.

"So, ah, did you all grow up in this area? Around Newthington?" Henry asked.

Enrico had his mouth stuffed full at the moment, but Paul glanced at him and answered, "Our family was from Old Bronx, originally. When we were babies, everyone moved down to Mexico—it was still just Mexico then—because of the war. After high school, I had come back up to New Yorkland as a student on a temporary permit, but Enrico and I had planned to leave Mexamerica permanently as soon as we could. Things were really locked down then, highest security. You couldn't go anywhere without facial ID. Lots of high capacity, fully automatic weapons—even in the groceries and schools. Shoot first, ask later. Funny, we left New York because things had gotten so bad, then had to leave Mexamerica because things were so bad there. Anyway, these two had just gotten married—" he gestured to Enrico and Pamela, who smiled broadly and made faces at each other, "—and there was a window in between one rigged election and the next. We took it."

Enrico swallowed. "Plus the heat, man. You didn't mention the heat. That's why we wanted to come up to the top of New Yorkland. Babe knows I just can't take those 120-degree summers anymore."

"Wow," Henry said. "You guys were really lucky to get a permit."

"Luck? Hah, not just that." Paul snorted. "Money. We sold everything we had, our father's land, cars, furniture, everything. *Then* we had to get lucky, too. I miss our friends and our family, but I'd do it again in a heartbeat."

"You got it, bro. Babe and me, we came up here to start a family." Enrico and Pamela squeezed each other's hands.

Henry smiled.

How nice for them. He'd never really wanted a family of his own. His sister, Lisa, had gone that route. Married, kids. But not Henry. *What if I turned into my dad? I'd never want to inflict that power-hungry control monster on anyone.*

Another ear-splitting peal of thunder rolled through the house, and it creaked and moaned. One of the LEDs dimmed and went out, its power supply exhausted.

"Hey, Enrico, want to grab some candles from that drawer? I don't think this other LED is going to last the night, not for all of us." Henry tried to keep the anxiety out of his voice.

Henry realized it had never been truly *dark* growing up and living in the megapolis. Not like this. As a kid, his dad admonished him not to be afraid of the dark, because there was nothing in the dark that wasn't there in the light.

Ha. Bullshit. Dad had never been to a place like this.

There were definitely things in the dark here. Things in the basement, in the shadows. Henry felt goosebumps, and the hair on his neck bristled.

Stop it, you're freaking yourself out again.

Paul and Enrico were lighting a handful of candles, setting them in holders.

Henry cleared the lump from his throat. "Er, I guess we might as well head to bed. Doesn't sound like the storm is going to let up any. Maybe get an early start tomorrow."

A draft from somewhere blew through and the candles wavered, their shadows bending and curving around the room.

"Yeah. Sure," Enrico said. They each took a candle or two and headed out through the ballroom to the grand staircase. They creaked their way up to the bedrooms, Henry turned to the left, the others to the right.

Pamela and Enrico took the first bedroom they found.

"Babe, you gotta be kidding me. There's crazy dust in here." Pamela stifled a sneeze. "Crazy."

Enrico patted the ancient mattress and made it cloudy in the room.

"And it's not like we can open the window!" She coughed a little.

"Yeah, the whole house needs some cleaning, too," Enrico admitted.

"You think?" Pamela scoffed. "I'll get started in daylight, but we might need some help. I can call Valéria; she's good."

"Sure, babe, sure." Enrico nodded. "We'll get this place all fixed up. Cleaned, patched, just like new!" He said it extra loud, almost as if it wasn't just for Pamela to hear.

Something flew past and banged into the window. Pamela jumped off the floor and held on to Enrico's shoulders.

"Just a bird, babe. Maybe a stick," Enrico said. "Nothing to worry about. I got you."

He really hoped he was right.

Henry tried to get comfortable, but sleeping was hard enough without the extra several pounds of cast on his arm. He was almost used to the unexplained noises at the house and wondered what the brothers and Pamela thought about it.

Bet they aren't sleeping either. He changed positions once more.

But he was happier than he had been, confident that these three and whatever helpers they needed could get the job done. With the house repaired and in good working order, maybe that was his biggest problem solved.

And as soon as you fix your biggest problem, your second biggest problem now becomes your biggest problem.

He rolled over again as much as he could.

But how do you fix a—

Even if there were such a thing as ghosts, even if the house is actually haunted, how do you even begin to fix it?

Is it even something that can be fixed?

Henry tossed and turned, and sleep gradually took him.

Twelve

A FIERCE BURP ERUPTED unexpectedly, echoing like a peal of thunder in the library building, which was otherwise quiet as a tomb.

Esmeralda poked her head out from behind the stacks. "J? Did you say something?"

"Ah, no, not really. Sorry. Don't get me wrong, I'm not unappreciative, but Pamela's cooking might actually kill me," said Henry, followed up by a few small gaseous aftershocks.

Esmeralda came over to his research table. "I wondered why you were spending so much time here this week. Feeling a little crowded up at Weatherly?"

"Yeah, I suppose so. Well, plus, they are professionals. I'm just in the way, and it's not like I can give them a *hand* or anything." He looked at his cast with a rueful expression.

"No pun intended, of course," Esmeralda noted.

"Of course," replied Henry.

"Memory reader working okay for you?" She gestured at the antique. "I can't remember the last time someone bothered to fire this thing up."

Which was just how Henry liked it, of course. This was an old machine that didn't have any sort of video conferencing built in, which meant no facial recognition, either. The more paranoid part of his brain suggested that it might have a microphone, though. But that was okay; he'd long been in the habit of drumming his fingers while typing, to throw off any audio or vibration sensing.

"Not much to go wrong with it, so yeah, working out just fine," Henry said, smiling slightly.

Esmeralda glanced at the stack of memory wafers, paperback, hardcover, and even a few leather-bound volumes. "You've been busy," she noted.

"Seemed a good opportunity to get out of the house for a while, catch up on some local history. History of the house and such."

Esmeralda nodded and moved on.

Henry poured over the texts for most of the day.

Many of the volumes dealt in some way with mining or early industrialization topics. Henry discarded most of those based on the titles alone. *Identification of Granite and Quartz Strata* did not hold out much hope of any useful information, and Henry tossed the volume aside. But on the shelf above, he found something that really grabbed his attention.

The Haunting of Shaft Seven: A True History of Eyewitness Accounts and Specialists in the Occult Arts was a hardcover book, with an embossed geometric design on the front cover and spine and faded, brittle, yellowed pages. They crinkled unpleasantly as Henry read though.

Like the skin on a dead man. Henry immediately regretted the macabre thought. But the text invited such thinking as he read through the horrors of that time.

It was the early 1900s, and the mines in the area were being worked hard. Too hard, as it turned out, and men and children were dying daily from accidents, neglect, and by the ruthless hand of one Ezekiel Sandor. "Zeke," as he was known, was the manager, or supervisor, of one of the local mines. And he didn't care who died or how, as long as quotas were met.

Henry couldn't believe the matter-of-factness of the jobs described in the book. Young children called *spraggers* would run alongside groaning mine carts as they sped downhill, sticking pieces of wood (*sprags*) into the turning wheels as temporary brakes. It was common for kids to be run over and crushed or have their hands or arms mangled and torn off.

In fact, any place you would expect to see a motor or an engine, a robotic arm or even just a simple mechanism, there was instead a small boy, or a large man as strength required. Zeke put them there and kept them there. Didn't matter to him if they got crushed, mangled, electrocuted, burned, or smothered. Zeke would shout at the remaining workers to "get the body out quick or you're next!"

And that was just the job end of it—the environment of the mine itself was another horror. Explosions were common, Henry read. They called them *firedamp*. A build-up of toxic gases that would explode, incinerating anyone in the way. Even if you survived the explosion itself, the carbon monoxide and other invisible gases of the *afterdamp* would suffocate you.

Explosions, cave-ins, toxic gases, and workers breathing so much particulate matter that you could see it on their breath when they exhaled. Many simply suffocated. Not that they needed to; many mines employed animals, such as mice or canaries, which are more sensitive to the poisonous gases and would give an early warning of problems in the mine.

But Zeke wouldn't buy mice or canaries. One worker recounted that Zeke thought anything like that was a waste of money. In fact, there were a lot of direct quotes from workers and townspeople about Zeke.

"Satan's right-hand man."

"Liked watching men die."

"If he didn' like ya, under the cart ya went."

And on it went. Clearly, a thoroughly despicable character. But that wasn't all. Death wasn't the end of the story, at least not in Shaft Seven. Henry leaned forward and hunched over the library table as he read the first-hand accounts:

"I saw him standing there, keen as day! I not be telling a thumper. 'Twas a bottom fact, for sure. And here he been dead nigh onto a week or more! But standing right in front of me he was. And me not very bricky, I shook right in my boots."

Henry didn't quite understand all the words or slang, but the meaning was clear enough. The next entry was more graphic.

"Robert reported seeing a phosphorescently glowing, translucent ectoplasmic manifestation, holding his pickaxe and wandering in the shaft, looking for a way out."

There was a lot of material here. He skimmed forward, picking up references to voices echoing in the mine, the words *get out* whispered menacingly in the dark corners. A ghostly lampman, handing out phantasmic lamps. Cries for help and murmured weeping from empty galleries and shafts. Shadowy mists blocking the way; dark shadows following the men. Oozing blood from the sinews of the rock itself.

Henry skipped back a page and re-read the section about dark shadows following the men, even when there was no light to cast them. A chill ran up his spine.

It sounded a lot like the basement at Weatherly. He kept reading.

The incidents got worse; miners reported ghostly hands grasping at them. In Shaft Seven, a fatal cave in killed a half-dozen miners. The few who survived said they saw faint, green glowing men with pickaxes clawing at the roof—causing the cave in. The men refused to enter the mines after that.

Zeke whipped them, screamed and threatened, but apparently, Zeke's whip wasn't as bad as certain death in the mine at the hands of vengeful spirits. In the midst of the hysteria, the screaming, and the whipping, a miner named William calmly suggested they conduct a séance—to listen to the spirits. Maybe make them go away.

Oddly enough, Zeke thought this was a reasonable idea. Perhaps he figured the séance would be a bust and convince the spooked men that there were no ghosts. At any rate, the whip alone wasn't working.

William was chosen to lead the séance, along with seven others. They went into the first gallery at the Shaft Seven site and set up a folding table with eight stools. A single gas lamp was placed in the center of the table, and the men held hands. The rest of the miners, along with Zeke, waited, and listened outside in the dark.

Henry turned the faded, crinkled page. The rustle seemed to echo in the library. He kept reading.

William had the men sit in a circle, hands held. "Do not let go, do not break the circle," he commanded them. In a low voice, he intoned an invitation to the spirit world. "Oh, spirits from beyond. We are here to speak and to listen. Show yourselves." Nothing happened for a great many minutes. William repeated the invitation, now loudly, now quietly. The men waited outside with great apprehension, watching the faint glow from the single lamp in the shaft.

Suddenly, there was a great silence over the land. The faint glow of the lamp was extinguished, and screams of terror filled the shaft. The men outside were rooted to the spot, afraid to go in and help their fellows and afraid to leave. After several tense minutes, the men came out of the shaft, in the dark yet walking assuredly all the same, as with common purpose. Not one said a word. In an instant, they seized old Zeke, that is, Ezekiel Sandor the manager, and they did lynch him there and then.

Henry blinked. He hadn't seen *that* coming.

A new man, Edward, was sent from the owners to manage the mine, and from that day, no hauntings or unexplained events were reported.

Henry flipped through the rest of the dry leaves of the book. There was no mention of any murder charges, no actions against the miners. But the hauntings stopped. He closed the book, set it on the table, leaned back in the creaky wooden chair, and sighed.

Maybe this was a genuine report of a real set of encounters with the supernatural. Maybe it was a fraud—a con set up by the miners to take out the evil manager. If so, how did they get away with it? Were people of that age really so superstitious and gullible? Did the authorities not care because it was just a bunch of miners? Or was it all, in fact, true? Some sort of sacrifice to avenge the wrongfully dead?

Esmeralda appeared suddenly, and Henry gave a slight jump.

"Reading ghost stories now, are we?" She nodded at the hardcover volume.

"Wha— oh, yeah. Well, local history, you know. At least it claims to be. Did they really think this stuff was true?" He looked up as Esmeralda, confusion on his face.

Esmeralda shrugged. "The miners and townspeople thought it was. Not for me to judge."

"I mean," Henry rolled his eyes and shoulders together, "ghosts and apparitions and ectoplasm and lynchings... What kind of crazy world *was* it?"

"Same crazy world it is today but better documented."

Henry raised his eyebrows. Esmeralda continued. "Enrico thinks Weatherly Hall is haunted. He thinks some evil spirit tried to attack him in the basement. And attacked you, too."

Henry looked off into the distance, then down at the table. "I know," he said quietly. "I mean, I know that's what Enrico thinks."

"And you?" Esmeralda asked. "What do you think?"

Henry took a deep breath. This really wasn't the conversation he wanted to have. "I... I don't know. I mean, I've seen some strange things, I guess, but it's a big drafty house. Lot of sounds and things I'm not used to. But there are no spectral apparitions, no ghosts. Just the house. How could it be haunted, if there even is such a thing, when there are no ghosts?"

Esmeralda pulled up a chair and sat. "The ancient Japanese had several belief systems that imbued inanimate objects with spirits. Shintoism, animism, perhaps a few others. I'm no expert, but they believed *everything* had a living spirit, not just human beings. There was even a cult in the early 21st century that worshiped folded clothes. *Kan-marie,* I think it was called."

Henry frowned. "What are you getting at?"

Esmeralda looked thoughtful. "The miners in that story. They talked to the spirits. Tried to help them, to find the source of their misery. Have you tried talking to the house?"

"What??" Henry half-asked, half-laughed. "You can't be serious."

Esmeralda did not smile. "Did you introduce yourself? Explain who you were, and why you were there?"

"No." Henry scowled. "Of course not. Who goes around *talking to houses*? Fiona would think I had a concussion. Well, she does anyway, but…" He trailed off.

"Enrico is pretty convinced there's a problem. That's why he's not alone in the house now."

"How do you know all this?" Henry asked.

"Small town," Esmeralda replied, smiling slightly. "Maybe there's nothing to it. Maybe Enrico is simply imagining things. And you as well. Perhaps the house is just a great anachronism, out of place and out of time. Maybe it should have been torn down after the war.

"But maybe you should try and… talk to it. Communicate your intentions. Other cultures held such beliefs, perhaps they knew something we didn't. There is no harm in trying." She shrugged her shoulders.

Henry tapped his fingers idly on the closed book. "No, I suppose there's no harm in trying."

––––––––––––––––––––

"Are you sure?" Enrico asked Paul.

"It's gotta be. You said so yourself, when you were tracing the wires."

"I know, man, but an axe? Seriously? Mr. J is gonna be real pissed if you're wrong." Enrico was emphatic.

"If I'm wrong, we patch the wall and don't even tell him. Okay?" Paul offered.

"Sure, I guess. But be gentle with it, okay? Like, man, don't hurt the house."

"What? What the hell do you mean?" Paul looked surprised.

"I mean, don't hurt it. Tell the house you're fixing it," Enrico insisted.

"Loco. You *loco*, man." Paul shook his head.

"Humor me, bro," Enrico countered.

"Fine. Okay. House, this doesn't belong here. Imma gonna fix it for you." Paul looked over at Enrico, exasperated. Enrico nodded.

Paul swung the axe at the wall, which yielded easily. Three more swings, and they could step through the opening.

"Holy shit," Paul said.

"Holy shit," Enrico echoed.

"Mr. J! You won't believe what we found!" Enrico greeted Henry at the door as he was returning from the library, words tumbling out of his mouth.

"Probably not," Henry agreed, his head still filled with the story of the miners and the haunted mine.

"We found the kitchen! The *real* kitchen. You gotta see this—man, it's huge. The stove is bigger than my first apartment."

Henry stood in the doorway, dumbfounded. "What?" he sputtered.

"The kitchen! You know that weird-looking wall in the kitchen, the one that doesn't match anything else in the house?" Enrico asked.

Henry nodded.

"We tore it down. The real kitchen is behind it. And I'm telling you, man, it's so huge! Never seen anything like it."

"You… tore down the wall?" Henry said with some concern.

Enrico looked a little offended. "Well, yeah, man. Needed to get to some wiring behind it. You still want the basement all fixed up, right?"

Henry nodded again, more cautiously this time.

"Well, we had to get in there. Only way." Enrico shrugged.

"So, you found a whole room? A hidden room?" Henry tried to wrap his head around it.

"Yeah, man. A kitchen. Huge. C'mon, I'll show you."

The "kitchen" that Henry had come to know was less than half of one section of the real kitchen. The other half was now exposed, which then went down a couple of room-wide steps to another section that was at least as large, featuring an immense stove built in to the curving outer wall of the house.

"Holy shit," Henry said.

"Yeah, man." Enrico nodded in agreement.

Thirteen

VALÉRIA HAD BEEN DUSTING BY HAND and started the vacuum bot to catch up behind her. The house was caked with dust, dead bugs, parts of desiccated spiders and millipedes, and the especially disgusting hellgrammites. Nasty-looking larvae with pincers and hairy antenna. Valéria shuddered as she swept up a crunchy pile of the bugs from under a heavy velvet drape.

She'd seen spider webs before but not like this. These were more like ropes than webs, thick and sticky. They rattled in the vacuum as she sucked them up, and she continued to shiver in disgust.

Pamela had offered her the job. She needed the money but almost said no anyway. She'd heard things about Weatherly from her parents and cousins. Rumors. During the war, the house was closed down and abandoned. But there were lights there at night, when there should not have been any.

And screams.

She had a vial of Holy Water that she'd gotten from her priest. She wouldn't say anything more than that she might need it. When Valéria first came to Weatherly earlier that week, she had sprinkled some at the doorway, then up the stairs. She had cleaned the piles of dust by the front door *every* time she passed. And as soon as she returned, the piles were back.

Madre de Dios. She crossed herself.

Nothing about this place was right. But she'd known Pamela, and her husband Enrico, for years now. They wouldn't drag her into anything dangerous on purpose.

On to the next bedroom. It was smaller, and the heavy, velvet-like wall hanging was tattered. Eaten by moths, by the look of it.

"Well, that won't do," she said, and started to tear the hanging down from the wall. "Out you go."

Pamela was helping Enrico clean up and paint in the kitchen when they heard Valéria's scream. Not a constant scream but a warbling, Doppler-shifted scream as she flung herself down the stairs and out the front door. Gravel flew as Valéria shot down the driveway and out of sight.

"What the hell?" Paul spat out, breathless as he ran up from the far side of the house. The three carefully climbed the stairs to the bedrooms where Valéria had been cleaning. All they saw was a sad wall hanging, half-torn from the wall, moth-eaten and threadbare.

And her shoes.

"Don't you think that's overkill?" Pamela asked as they headed down the long, dark stairs to the basement.

"No way, it's worked every time so far, sweetie," Enrico replied under his breath. "We even tore down a wall, and nothing tried to kill us."

"Tell that to Valéria," Pamela muttered.

In a louder, calm, and reassuring voice, Enrico spoke to the darkness. "Hey. We're here to help. Get you all cleaned up. Fixed up, working. Just like you like. We'll take care of you. Not gonna hurt you… yeah, we're on your side. Clean you up nice. You let us know what you need, we'll take of it…" He kept on in a soothing voice as he got to the bottom of the stairs. Enrico fired up the lighting rig, and the basement was filled with pure white light.

"I think I'm getting a tan, baby," Pamela muttered.

"Shh…" Enrico jerked his head back at her, then swiped on his panel and festive bright music erupted with guitars, violins, and trumpets.

Pamela raised her eyebrow at Enrico. "That's Javier Solís, sweetie. The best!" Enrico beamed as the vocals came in.

The music was upbeat, happy, with an infectious beat. Enrico had been playing it—along with enough light to probably cause a sunburn—every time he had gone down in the basement.

They walked together, holding hands, down the center of the basement to the far wall with the shiny new electrical panel.

"Don't get me wrong, baby, I like holding hands and all, but is this really—" Pamela started.

"Yes! Shhhh! It's worked so far." Enrico got to the panel and opened it.

Pamela frowned. "Looks different from normal houses."

"Yeah, this is old-school. Power only, no data. J wanted it that way. Keeping with the house, I guess." He flicked a breaker, took a measurement, checked a few things. "Look, here—I even put in a data filter on the powerline, to prevent any data *exfiltration*." He smiled, smugly. Pamela started pacing, walking around the absurdly brightly-lit basement.

Enrico fiddled with a connector while Pamela started exploring the entrances to the storerooms and hallways branching off the main basement.

"Hey, don't go too far, sweetie. Stay here in the light, in the main hall, yeah?"

"Yeah, okay, baby," Pamela replied off-handedly as she peered down the increasing gloom of a side passage. This room had meat hooks on the wall and a large drain in the floor.

"Sweet Jesus, save us," she whispered. "It's a freaking torture chamber!"

She screamed as she felt the hand on her shoulder.

"Whoa, baby, it's just me!" Enrico instinctively ducked.

Pamela swatted at him anyway. "What kind of freaky house *is* this?" she demanded.

"I dunno, sweetie. How many kinds of freaky houses are there these days? It's one of those," Enrico said.

"Smartass. This room was built to torture people! Hang them by hooks and bleed them out! Look!"

Enrico shook his head. "Well, maybe. More likely this is where they prepped deer and other shit they shot for dinner."

Pamela glared at him.

"This whole basement has rooms for all kinds of food storage and prep. All kinds of weird, bad-ass shit down here. They didn't have stores or food drones or nothin' back then. You wanted meat, you had to shoot it and peel it and dress it yourself!"

Pamela shuddered. "Gross."

Enrico shrugged. "Maybe that's why everyone gets freaked out down here. But I don't think so. I think the house was scared of us. Like a strange dog—it barks and yips at you until you pet it, tell him he's a good boy, then he's your bud."

"So, babe, you think the house is a dog?" Pamela gave him a look.

"No, not a dog. *Like* a dog. Like a kid. Like a scared kid who thinks you're going to hurt it. We just have to keep telling the house it's okay. It's going to be okay. We're here to help."

Pamela rolled her eyes and headed for the stairs. "Hey, whatever works. Mr. J is paying well, and we need the money, so if you have to give the house a freaking birthday present wrapped in polka dots, I'm okay with that. Whatever it takes."

Enrico laughed as they headed back upstairs.

———————————

"You want to try *what*?" Pamela asked, eyes wide. Henry, Pamela, and the brothers Enrico and Paul were sitting in the kitchen at Weatherly.

"A séance," Henry said. "You know, like in the old movies. We all sit around a table in the dark with candles at midnight and try and communicate with the spirit world."

Paul and Enrico looked at each other with alarm. Pamela rolled her eyes, and asked, "Are you crazy? Have you ever been treated for, you know, mental things?"

Henry scowled. "I was diagnosed with depression, once."

Enrico jumped in. "By a real doctor, or just the algorithms?"

"Implants. I had them removed after that, said I couldn't afford the subscription."

Paul threw up his hands. "Okay, so let's assume you're *not* actually crazy, and maybe Enrico really did encounter... something... in the basement. And Valéria encountered something upstairs. Did she say—?"

"She's not speaking to me and won't talk about it," Pamela grumbled.

"Great. Well, even if there's something going on here, sitting around holding hands in the dark isn't going to fix anything!"

Henry nodded. "Look, Enrico has been going around talking to the house, treating it like a scared animal or something, and it seems to be working. There's still weird things happening, but we haven't had any serious accidents or problems since I got back from the hospital. So this is the next logical step. I read this book at the library about a haunted mine shaft in town. Worse problems than we had here, and once they held a séance and straightened out the problem, the hauntings stopped."

They sat in silence for a few minutes.

Enrico spoke first. "What would we have to do, man?"

"Just what you've been doing—talk to the house. But more direct. With all of us. We'd… we'd ask the house to talk back to us."

Enrico jumped up from the table. "Now just hang on there, Mr. J! Whatever we're doing is working. The house isn't trying to kill us today, man. I don't want to screw with that. What if it gets mad at us? Valéria… man, she was just cleaning, and then… well, I don't know what, but she got the hell out and ain't coming back." He looked around nervously and quickly sat back down.

Henry thought a minute and quietly answered, "And what if we accidentally do something else to make the house mad? Without knowing it? Wouldn't it be better if we could, you know, talk to it? Find out?"

Paul leaned back and threw his hands up. "You guys *are* crazy. Both of you. Diagnostics be damned. You're talking about this house like it's a person, like a living thing. *It's just a house.* It's not alive. There's nothing here to talk to! Crazy. *Loco!*" He shook his head.

"Maybe," Henry admitted. "But you've got to agree, you two have gotten all this work done, including all the electrical and heating work in the basement, without any of the attacks and weird shit we had going on."

"Could be a coincidence." Paul shrugged again. "Or maybe with all of us here, we scared off whatever wild attack squirrel was living in the basement."

"Okay." Henry kept at it. "If there's nothing to it, then a séance won't hurt anything. Nothing here to answer. No harm, no foul. But if there is some kind of… something… here, then we should try to talk to it better."

"So what's so special about a séance, then?" Pamela asked. "Why can't Enrico just keep petting the house and telling it nice things?"

Enrico scowled at the characterization but didn't say anything.

"I don't know." Henry shrugged. "Maybe nothing. But I've been reading a lot at the library on this kind of stuff, and this is what people do. At least, it's what they used to do. And it fixed their weird problems. I think we should try it."

Paul looked around the table. "Okay. Fine. What do we have to do?"

Henry fixed his gaze on each one of them, slowly, before replying, "Have an open mind."

———————

McBurk had waited, more or less patiently, until his monitor picked up the discharge notice for his subject. For reasons he still couldn't understand, the subject was only referred to as "J" on all documents he had access to.

I can't even figure out this guy's real name, he fumed. *But I'm about to find out a whole lot more.*

The fleet of three small, highly maneuverable, manual drones were heading up the long driveway to Weatherly, launched from what looked like a common garbage bot out on the main road.

He had to get separate authorization for the manual scan, which had been a little tricky. There was no cause, nothing to point directly to any illegal activity. Suspicious, yes, but nothing illegal.

And the regular drone scans hadn't helped his case. They continued to show nothing. Maybe J hadn't gone back to work yet and was staying somewhere else? McBurk wondered at that.

So his request for higher-precision, stealthy, manual drones was met with raised eyebrows. The deliberately confusing chain of custody was all he could offer, all he had to go on. It wasn't really enough, but McBurk persisted until he got official approvals.

The three drones approached the driveway.

I'll get you now, you sonofabitch. He grinned with anticipation. McBurk prepared to drive the drones right up to the windows, coming in from the east with the sun behind them.

SOFTWARE FAILURE. ERROR CODE 5103. RE-TURNING TO BASE AT LAST KNOWN POSI-TION.

The drones' video feeds all went dark, and data and telemetry stopped updating.

"What. The. FUCK!" McBurk bellowed, veins in his pink neck bursting with purple.

He slammed the desk with his fist, punched at the controllers, but nothing happened. He had no control over the drones now; they would automatically return and dock. Not only had the mission failed, but he'd have to file the equipment report explaining exactly what he was doing and why, and try and make it clear that *he'd* done nothing wrong to damage the drones. By then, the original authorization for the drones would have expired. So no evidence, just lots of useless forms and reports to fill out.

By the book.

"Fuck, fuck, FUCK!" he repeated, slamming back in his chair.

Another officer, Reynolds, was walking past. She ducked her head in to say, "You know, you are going to stroke out if you keep acting out like that."

McBurk barely looked at her as he fumed. "Fuck you too, Grace."

Reynolds smiled kept walking down the hall. *Yeah, he's not going to last very long.* She smiled at the thought.

Weatherly was in top form that evening, with a magnificent, slow rolling thunderstorm cracking across the treetops.

"What the hell is up with thunderstorms this late in the season?" Paul grumbled.

"Atmosphere." Pamela grinned as she set up the candles. Her fine, silken hair reflected the insufficient light. They had set up a square table in the middle of the ballroom, with four chairs and four candles, one for each of them. It was nearing midnight and they were almost ready.

"So, like, what do we *do*, man?" Enrico repeated as they took their seats. Pamela cut off the remaining LEDs and joined them.

"An open mind," Henry repeated. "Well, not just open but… empty. Clear your minds of distractions. Don't think about the day's events, don't plan for tomorrow, don't try to guess what's going to happen. Just think about, well, nothing. Focus on the candle flame." He nodded to the center of the table.

The four candle flames cast the only light in the cavernous ballroom. Shadows of their forms danced on the walls, grotesquely enlarged. Lightning flashed off in the distance, followed by the slow, growling rumble of thunder. But the storm was a ways off still.

"Okay, everyone, hold hands now," Henry instructed. They joined hands, forming a circle. "Repeat after me, and keep chanting the chant. Don't say anything else, and don't stop, and don't let go."

Henry took a deep breath and chanted in a flat monotone, "Spirits of the past, move among us. Be guided by the light of this world and visit upon us."

He paused. Nodded at the others.

"Spirits of the past, move among us. Be guided by the light of this world and visit upon us," the four said, more or less in unison.

Pause.

"Spirits of the past, move among us. Be guided by the light of this world and visit upon us."

Lightning arced in the woods, the thunder cracked almost at the same time. Pamela startled but didn't let go.

"Spirits of the past, move among us. Be guided by the light of this world and visit upon us."

On they went, staring at the flickering candles, chant, pause, chant, pause. Every so often, thunder would bark in the distance, lightning would flash and fill even the dark corners of the ballroom with bright but fleeting light.

The pauses between chants grew longer, the candles burned down shorter, and the clock crept up on one in the morning.

"So… how long do we do this, bro?" Enrico asked.

Pamela kicked him under the table. "Babe, don't break the chant!"

Henry jumped in. "No, it's okay. It's not working. We've been at this almost an hour. Something should have happened by now." He let his hands go, breaking the circle, and leaned back in his chair. "I really thought…" He trailed off.

Silence. Still, oppressive.

"Hey, hang on, lemme try," Enrico said. "Hands together, come on." They reformed the circle.

"Oh, spirit of the house. Oh, Weatherly. We have come to help you. To fix you, like I said. Help us. Let us know what you want. We'll do our best, man. Tell us what you need."

All four involuntarily looked up into the darkness of the balcony encircling the ballroom, to the ceiling above, and then down to each other.

Silence.

Henry shrugged and started to let go, but Enrico shook his head vigorously. No. Not yet.

They waited.

A distant, weak peal of thunder from the trailing edge of the storm echoed far in the distance.

"Well, that's that." Henry let go and stood up, dejected. He walked across the ballroom and turned the lights on. Pamela blew out the candles.

"You two can start on the greenhouse in the morning," Henry said softly. "I'd like to make sure the whole house is buttoned up tight before winter sets in."

"Sure thing, man, you got it," Enrico said.

Henry walked them out, locked the big front door behind them, and sighed at the two large piles of ash by the front door.

Henry sat in the breakfast room, sipping a cup of hot tea, at his new small, polished oak table. Despite the fact that the kitchen was now three times its original size, he still used the small stove to heat up water for tea. The giant stove would take some research and maybe a forest's worth of trees to fire up before he could use it.

Normally, it would be brightly lit and sunny in the morning in the breakfast room, but today was gray and cloudy out. A gust of chill wind made the house shudder.

He absently stirred honey into his tea, clinking the cup loudly in the still and quiet.

It should have worked. It should have worked…

He slammed the spoon onto the table and leaned back.

On the one hand, whatever Enrico was doing seemed to be working, at least a little. Nothing dangerous had happened in the basement, or anywhere else. But things were far from normal still. Doors still slammed for no reason, the piles of ash still reappeared at the front door, and the nightmares… Henry shuddered and took a sip of tea.

The nightmares were as bad as ever, maybe even getting worse. Whatever was wrong with the house… it was still wrong. Unlike the haunted mineshaft, there was no evil manager to kill. This house had sat empty for enough time that any bad guys were long dead or moved on. Henry frowned. What could he possibly do to avenge some wrong from long ago? To make the house at peace?

Like in the graveyard. Resting, in peace.

Resting.

In peace.

Not in piles by the door or in the trash.

Henry jumped up, a new idea taking root in his head quickly.

First stop was in the newly-cleaned up and rebuilt greenhouse. Enrico and Paul had cleaned it out, repaired the broken glass, and got it ready for a new generation of plantings. Pamela started Henry off with a couple of tomato and squash seedlings. They were small still but seemed vibrant with life. Henry smiled at the thought and picked up what he came for: a small, hand-sized shovel.

He left the greenhouse through the glass door, down the short stone stairs to the yard and headed downhill to the graveyard. The wind whipped around him, and he regretted not putting on a heavier coat. Past the outbuildings, he approached the family graveyard.

Henry found a nice spot by the thin, wrought-iron fencing, knelt onto the cold, hard ground and cleared away leaves and debris with his hands and the edge of the shovel. Next he dug a hole, carefully saving the dirt in a neat pile.

He left the shovel and went back up to the house. Rummaging around in the kitchen, he found a metal bowl and a solid spatula. Back out through the ballroom to the entrance hall, he knelt and gently scooped up the first pile of ash into the bowl, then the second. Grabbing a coat this time from the adjacent cloak room, he headed down the windy hill to the graveyard.

Slowly, he poured the ash into the freshly dug hole and tapped the bowl to loosen the last few bits. Setting the bowl down, he re-filled the hole with dirt, and tamped it down. Henry stood up and looked around. He wasn't *exactly* expecting anything to happen.

Maybe I should say something. Like a prayer.

He thought a minute, then gazed up at the gray and leaden sky, at a loss for words. Trying to remember dialog at funeral scenes from movies and books, he finally said, "May the souls of the departed find rest—eternal rest— here. Send angels to watch over this grave, and protect it from all evil. Let light perpetual shine upon the honored dead. May these souls rest in peace."

Henry looked around again, just in case, and then slowly walked back up to the house.

What the hell am I doing, Henry wondered as he past the outbuildings. He poked his head into the ice house and checked on the drone countermeasures, and especially the powercells. Everything seemed in order.

Burying dirt. Like that's going to change anything. Shit, this place is getting to me. Henry shook his head and kicked at the gravel as walked across the driveway.

The door groaned with annoyance as Henry entered the house. Warily, he glanced at the corners in the entrance hall. No ash had returned yet, but usually it took a while to build up. He wandered in the large drawing room at the rear of the house and spent more than a few minutes just looking out over the grounds and across the rippling hills in the distance.

Such a beautiful spot. So quiet and lovely. If this house wasn't just so damn weird, so…

Haunted.

Henry turned angrily, refusing to even think the word. And yet here he was, burying mysterious piles of ash and spraying bright light and music into the basement to chase off the bogeyman. He passed through the breakfast room and ducked into the billiard room. He hadn't spent much time in here yet, but Paul had gotten the table fixed up and smooth again, with a full complement of billiard balls and cues. Henry chucked a ball down the field and into a pocket.

Back out through the gymnasium at the front of the house, he made his way back to the entrance hall.

Shit. He forced himself to look in the corners to see if the ash had returned. *What if, but what, that is…* His mind raced.

Clenching his jaw, he walked up the hall and deliberately looked in the corners.

There, in the corner in the hallway, was—

Nothing.

No ash. He turned around and looked in the other corner. Nothing.

Holy shit. Maybe it worked?

It was time to head down to the library. Henry had a really good feeling that he was making progress.

Fourteen

"I THOUGHT YOU MIGHT APPRECIATE THIS," Esmeralda said as she handed Henry a very old book, bound in a hardcover but looking remarkably fresh.

Not read much. Henry took it and looked at the cover: *A Local History of Southfield.* "What's Southfield?" he asked.

"This end of town. Before it became part of Newthington in the mid 1900s. There's a whole section on Weatherly Hall. I marked it for you."

Henry tipped the book and saw a ribbon bookmark dangling from the pages. He looked at the cover again. "What was Southfield south of?"

Esmeralda shrugged. "Nothing, as far as I can tell. Just a name."

"Thanks, I'll take a look."

Esmeralda nodded and silently swept off to another part of the library.

Henry sat at a long table with his growing pile of books on local history, mining, the occult, a few books on psychology—not many of those survived, however. That had been a popular topic for book burning after the war.

This war. Just the latest, Henry mused as settled in and got comfortable. *A Local History of Southfield* was about a different time, after a different war, the First Civil War in the mid-1800s.

The description of the area was familiar, but richer, more picturesque. One passage mentioned the abundance of wildlife, including *fields and woods teeming with many white deer.*

White deer. Huh. Henry flipped the page and thought about the one white deer that had almost ended his whole adventure before it began. *Hard to imagine the place crawling with them, or lots of any wildlife, really.* There were plenty of birds, still, and apparently at least a few coyotes. But it had been decades since the land "teemed" with anything.

Pastoral descriptions aside, he gently lifted the ribbon bookmark and skipped ahead to the section on Weatherly Hall:

A wondrous palace of joy and laughter, standing tall and mighty on its hill in defence against the weather of the world.

Henry read some basic details, some of which he'd already come across. Mr. Ferguson, who'd built Weatherly, owned a couple of factories and a few smaller mines in the area. But instead of being aloof, sealed up in his mansion, he was known for his hospitality and generosity. Large parties were common and invitations easy to come by.

Those were better times, Henry mused. But he realized that war was war. Apparently, during and after the First Civil War, the vast basements at Weatherly were used to house, feed, and care for runaway slaves from the Southern Confederacy at the time. The town of Southfield was far enough north that there wasn't much actual fighting going on, but as with any war, there were displaced people and refugees to manage. And Weatherly rose to the challenge.

But there were rumors, too, that Ferguson had a liking for the young ladies, and could "magically" appear in the upstairs guest bedroom without being seen.

You sneaky bastard. Henry grinned. *You put in a secret passage, didn't you?* Henry made a mental note to look into that.

After all, the guys just found a huge kitchen that had been boarded up and forgotten. Who knows what else we'll find?

He read for much of the day, dusted some books, and helped Esmeralda move several boxes of books off the sagging, crumbling shelves that had been their homes for many years and into storage. The weak sun was shuffling down to the horizon when he left for The Grumpy Yorkie.

Fiona was there already, waiting for him at a table near the front. A violent gust of wind caught the door just as Henry came in, slamming it loudly behind him.

So much for a quiet entrance. Henry looked sheepish. Only a few heads turned to the door, but one of them was the pink psycho cop. Henry pretended not to notice and slipped into the chair by Fiona, which creaked loudly.

"Well, Dr. Shelton, what a pleasant surprise."

She nodded and sipped her wine. "Good to see you, too, J. How's the arm doing since we took the cast off?"

"Pretty good." Henry rubbed it, mostly unconsciously. "I've been staying away from any heavy lifting or activity. Letting the guys have all the fun. They got into it with some axes the other day."

Fiona raised both eyebrows. "Axes? In the house? I thought Pamela was going to keep you fellows from doing stupid shit like that. I'll have to have a word with her. I have enough patients to deal with as it is. Bad week for overdoses." She took a longer drag on the wine glass.

"No, it was okay, it was cool," Henry said as Reginald came over. "Beer. Cold."

Reginald nodded and continued his circuit back to the bar.

"They discovered a boarded-up room and opened it up."

"Holy shit," Fiona said, a little too loudly. She leaned in. "What was in it? What did you find?"

"A kitchen. Well, *the* kitchen. The famous, extra-huge kitchen of Weatherly. Not like buried treasure or anything." Henry smiled.

Fiona did not. She waited until Reginald had delivered the generic but well-chilled beer and gone back. She leaned in even closer. "Listen. You need to be careful what you start opening up."

Henry smiled wider, "Oh, so you've bought in to the ghost story now, have you?" He took a big gulp of the beer.

"Not that. Well, not really." She lowered her voice to a whisper and leaned in. "But I have heard things about Weatherly that you should know." She looked around the bar quickly. "But not here. Finish your beer first." She leaned back and said in a louder voice, "Glad to hear you are staying off the arm, taking care of yourself."

They finished their drinks and quietly slipped out the door. Henry was sure he felt McBurk's beady little eyes boring into him as he left. Out in the parking lot, Fiona pulled him aside and spoke very quietly.

"Listen, J. I get to hear things. Lots of things that ordinary people don't. Things that don't get posted, don't get shared. That aren't known. Remember at the height of the war, when the Resist Movement leaders all disappeared?"

Henry shook his head. "Fled. They cashed out, took all the money, and fled to United China."

Fiona looked at the ground. "No. That was the story, and that's the official record, but that's not what happened. They were killed. All of them. Tortured and killed, here, at Weatherly."

"Wha—" Henry started to splutter. "That's crazy. And no way they could have covered that up."

"No? There are no genetic scanners up this far. No cameras on the road, if you know what routes to take. They control the satellites, so no worries there."

Henry rolled the idea over in his mind. *I mean, maybe…*

She continued. "I'm just saying, it's very likely that Weatherly was used as some kind of black ops site during the war. Who knows what they may have left behind—accidentally or on purpose. Bioweapons? Toxins that make you hallucinate? Forbidden tech? Could be anything. I just want you to be careful. Don't go digging up anything that's better off buried."

Henry's thoughts tumbled all over each other, each trying to get out of his mouth first. "But… but if any of that is true, people need to know."

"Do they?" Fiona asked, bitterness dripping from each syllable. "The truth died in the war, remember? People don't care about who, or where, or why. They care about getting on with their lives and not getting caught."

"Caught doing what?" Henry asked.

"Anything," Fiona replied, backing away suddenly.

McBurk was storming out the door of The Grumpy Yorkie toward them. Henry braced himself. The verbal assault was one thing, but the stench from McBurk's breath was far worse.

"You! Jay! Hold up. I gots some thingss t'ask youse." His words were slurred, eyes having difficulty focusing.

"Evening, Officer… McBurk, isn't it?" Henry pretended to struggle remembering his name.

"You know fuck well I am, you little turd. I've flushed bigger crooks than you before breakfast when I worked Central." He hiccupped, coughed, and made a few other bio-expulsions all at once.

"And now you're going to tell me your name. Your *full* name, Mr. 'J'." He swayed a bit in the cold night air, fog from his breath wafting over his pink features.

"Are you on duty, Officer McBurk?" Fiona asked.

McBurk only now glanced over at her. "No, *Dr.* Shelton, I am obviously *not* on duty, I—"

"Then we'll say goodnight to you, sir." Henry nodded and started to back away.

"The *fuck* you will, you shit. I'll unzip right here and beat it out of you with my great big—"

"Eric."

Both Henry and Fiona looked past McBurk quickly and gestured. McBurk whipped around to see Reginald and a few of the bar regulars standing right there.

"Eric," Reginald repeated. "Not here. We've talked about this. You need to go home now." Reginald spoke calmly but firmly, as one would to a misbehaving toddler.

"Fuck you too, Reg," McBurk raged.

"Now, Eric." Reginald was firm.

McBurk fumed, but there were witnesses. Too many. And Reginald was his only source of old Kentucky bourbon. He left without another word.

Fiona breathed a sigh and relaxed. Henry thanked her for drinks and left quickly. He had a lot to think about.

As he entered the great hall at Weatherly, he stole a quick glance down at the corners where the mysterious ash kept appearing.

No ash.

The front hall was clean.

Henry sat alone in the great ballroom. Most of the work had been completed, and Enrico, Paul, and Pamela were no longer underfoot. As much as he'd grumbled at having them around, Weatherly seemed empty and lonely without them.

Maybe the séance worked. Or the burial. The house felt… different. Maybe not exactly normal, or peaceful, yet, but definitely different. Henry took that to be progress.

He'd gotten a Christmas tree—an actual live tree, not artificial or laser display. That had been an adventure all to itself, trekking out into a field of trees to select one that would be just the right size and shape, then having the workers cut it down with a portable, hydrogen-powered saw. Henry felt like he'd finally and truly left the megapolis behind and was "one of the locals." A fresh tree, just cut! Not like one of those sad, brown desiccated trees you could sometimes find on the outskirts.

Still, the small, drought-stricken Douglas Fir was already shedding needles. In the quiet of the grand ballroom, he could hear the needles tinkle as they hit the polished floor.

Not quite sleigh bells. He took a sip of the whiskey he'd gotten, a fine single-malt scotch, and looked around the room. *This must have been quite the place back in its day.* He imagined all the lights lit, a roaring fire in the huge stone fireplace, room full of revelers, champagne flowing freely while a small live band played cocktail jazz versions of all the Christmas classic tunes. Filled with happy, outgoing people. Now, just one morose person.

He took another, healthier sip. *It was the right move.* There was no use second-guessing it. Had he stayed in the megapolis, he would have been discovered. It was just a matter of time, and not much time at that. He looked through the bottom of the glass, watched it distort the firelight into a flickering ring. Like a kaleidoscope. A colorful ring of yellow fire played around the edge of the glass.

And then he saw a face in the reflection.

Pale, with slicked back, jet black hair.

The fuck! Heart pounding, blood slamming into his head for an instant headache, Henry dropped the glass and whipped around.

He was alone.

He blinked, looked around again. Nothing. Just the quiet tinkle of pine needles pinging against the floor every few minutes.

Another restless night as sleep darted just out of reach. Henry lay in the giant bed in the equally grand master bedroom, listening to the full panoply of nighttime noises. Dark shadows crossed the windows, sounds of desperate children crying in the woods—but he knew these were only bats, birds, coyotes, and all the rest of very normal, explainable wildlife.

The face in the ballroom, though, that was another matter.

I was tired. I was drinking. Just my imagination. He tried to convince himself of that convenient lie, but he knew in his heart he *had* seen something. Something that was not a bat, coyote, or crow. Something in the house.

Despite his worry, he dropped off to sleep quickly enough.

And the ballroom was filled with people, happy celebrants of life. Henry knew he was dreaming, which was unusual for him. He tried to guide the dream, tried to make himself known and talk to anyone in the sea of faces.

But it was as if *he* was the ghost. They all carried on about their business, oblivious to his very existence. He tried to knock things over, tried to grab a man by the arm—anything to get their attention. But nothing worked. They just carried on with their party, their lives.

Tears welled up. He beat his fists in frustration. But nothing worked; the ballroom guests ignored his every effort.

He woke up with a start, in the black silence of his bedroom.

Only, the bedroom wasn't exactly the same as he'd left it. The silk wallpaper was clean and shiny; the windows perfectly crystal clear. The cracks in the ceiling were gone. Everything looked shiny and new. And he wasn't alone.

There was a figure in the bed next to him.

Used to the nightmares he'd been having, Henry flung himself off the bed onto the floor. But something was different—this time the covers did not come with him or tangle him up.

What the fuck…?

The figure in the bed rolled over and snored lightly. But instead of the usual half-dismembered, bloody visions he'd been seeing lately, this was a youngish woman. Beautiful, with long, flowing, jet-black hair and ivory skin.

Henry took a closer look at the room. A candle in its stand stood by the bedside. Piles of quilts covered the bed—thick, warm, suited for a harsh winter in an unheated building. How had he jumped out of bed without bringing all that with him?

He reached to pick up the candle, and his hand passed right through it.

FUCK.

He jumped back a pace, startled. The woman in the bed did not seem to notice.

He took a step closer to the bed and tried to lift up the covers. Again, his hand passed right through.

"Shit!" he yelled.

Nothing.

Confused, Henry walked over to the closed door that led back into the dressing room. He tried to grab the doorknob and couldn't.

Henry steeled himself, took a deep breath, closed his eyes, and deliberately walked right into the door.

And found himself in the dressing room. He turned around, staring at the very solid door he had just *walked right through*. Henry crossed the opulent, sparkling, and noticeably clean dressing room and through another solid door out into the hall. He walked down the hallway with silent footsteps and poked his head right into the wall to look into the adjacent bedroom.

A pair of figures were huddled under the blankets and quilts. He looked around the room quickly, it was just as clean and fresh as his own bedroom. He pulled his head out of the wall and continued on.

Bedroom after bedroom, he kept on. The house was filled with people, sleeping peacefully in quiet opulence. Henry made his way out to the balcony and looked down at the fading fire in the great fireplace in the ballroom.

A Christmas tree stood proud in the middle of the ballroom, right where he'd placed his own. But this one was decorated differently. Simple, folksy. Henry glided silently—didn't walk—down the staircase to the ballroom to look at it. He made it over to just about the same position he'd been in, back in his version of Weatherly, when he noticed the man.

He jumped back a pace, in spite of himself. But there, standing in the ballroom, was a man with very pale skin and jet black, slicked-back hair. He was dusting the mantle and didn't seem to notice Henry.

After his initial shock, Henry studied the man more closely. Formal attire, black trousers and coat with long tails, white shirt, very stiff looking, with some kind of embellishment at the front of the neck. He waved his hand in front of the man's face, yelled in his ear, and ran his hand right through him.

Nothing.

Henry looked back toward the tree and saw his chair— at least, a similar chair, in a similar position in front of the Christmas tree. Maybe it was a hunch, maybe it was wishful thinking, but he crossed the room and sat in the chair, assuming the position he had been in before this waking nightmare.

The world folded in on itself, a kaleidoscope of light and dark, energy and spirit, and with a thunderous roar that echoed into the still night, Henry found himself back in his ballroom, wan firelight and the quiet tinkle of pine needles pinging against the floor.

He sat there, muscles clenched hard against the chair, until the thin, grasping hands of daylight tore the dark apart.

———

Henry greeted the dawn, shaking visibly, red eyes aching, unable to close them.

He stood slowly, tentatively, afraid that reality would shatter around him again, his mind reeling with a thousand questions.

Who were those people? Who was that guy? WHEN were all those people? Was I in their world or they in mine? Am I going crazy?

As his thoughts jumbled and crashed into each other, one memory stood out from his reading at the library— ghosts did not infiltrate this world, as was commonly thought.

They dragged you into theirs.

Fifteen

Henry sat glumly in the breakfast room.

Well, that proves it. Either there really are ghosts, or I've gone insane.

Neither prospect was pleasant.

He puttered around the house, cleaning, dusting, fixing up some of the odds and ends leftover since Enrico and Paul had finished their work. But he felt listless, exhausted, spent.

The burner phone he used to contact Enrico and company rang, an incongruous, electronic chirp in an otherwise tomb-like silence.

Cautiously, he picked up the phone and pressed "answer."

"Henry? It's Lisa."

What the actual fuck?

Henry hadn't spoken to his sister in… years, at least. Not due to any particular drama; they'd just grown apart and didn't really have anything in common anymore.

Both parents were long dead; they lived in different countries now. Lisa had married, had produced a couple of children. *Three or four?* Henry was embarrassed that he didn't really remember. Or care.

"Lisa?"

"Hey, I know it has been a while, but we need to talk. I have been trying to find you, but you were not in your apartment anymore. I followed you up here. Can you come into town and meet me at the Quick Creek Motel?"

Henry hung up immediately and flung the phone to the floor, looking frantically for something to smash it with. He grabbed a particularly heavy lamp with a cast-iron base and smashed the phone. He'd get another one out of the box.

That wasn't Lisa.

His breath came ragged, choppy. *That was an AI simulation.* He could tell. The subtle high-frequency chirps, the microsecond pauses that most people wouldn't notice. The cadence. The vocabulary. All of it. Close, but not quite right.

It wasn't his sister.

But it was someone who *knew* him. The AI was programmed to greet him with his real name, Henry. Not J, as he'd been known locally. And somehow knew how to find him. Here. Despite his precautions.

Henry reeled and dashed through to the front of the house, half-expecting to see drones flying up the driveway. It was clear. He grabbed his coat and went out past the outbuildings and sheds to check on the anti-drone equipment. All was operating fine.

He breathed a short sigh of relief and hurried back inside. Drones or not, there were still satellites.

I have to go into town. Try and set up a tap on the police station, see what they have on me.

It was risky, and that sort of thing wasn't Henry's specialty. He'd need to get a few more pieces of equipment from a dead drop, which was an added risk all by itself.

Henry wandered in through the hall and smiled ever so slightly at the lack of mysterious piles of ash.

I guess the problems of the next world are easier to fix than the problems of this world. Henry sighed.

He made it to the kitchen table, sat, and pulled out a sheaf of paper and an old-fashioned graphite pencil from the drawer.

He started making lists. And plans.

———

Henry felt better; he had a plan. It was risky, but it was important to do some reconnaissance, to know what the police had on him, what they were planning. He felt well-protected from drone surveys, but that was only the first step. If armed forces arrived at the door, he had no capacity to resist.

Arms dealers were an option, but that really wasn't his thing. You could buy all the guns you could possibly afford and still wouldn't come close to the standard armory of even a small-town sheriff. That just wasn't a fight you could ever expect to win, despite the historical successes of figures like Rambo and other revolutionaries.

No, if it came to that, his only option was to flee. Run, run away, run fast. Where? Canada's border was heavily guarded and ridiculously well-armed to keep out refugees, especially since the border had been pushed so far north during the war. That probably wasn't viable. Henry frowned. His options were limited. He'd put everything into this move, this escape.

This has to work.

He had to throw the idiot locals off his trail before they got the professionals involved.

He was mulling that over when he heard a knock at the door.

Argh, probably Enrico. He and Paul had said they'd stop by sometime to finish up a few loose ends. Hurriedly, he shoved his papers into the drawer and went back to the front of the house to answer it.

He opened the massive door with a groan, and McBurk fired his stun gun at point-black range.

Henry hit the floor with a thud, shock and surprise frozen on his face, drool starting to leak out of his frozen, open mouth.

"Got you, fucker." McBurk stepped over Henry and closed the door behind him.

"White deer, huh. I ran over one of those fucking things last season. Put a big-ass dent in my truck," McBurk ranted at the floor design as he dragged Henry's frozen body out of the hallway. Just in case someone else came to the door. But in the middle of the grand ballroom, McBurk groaned.

"Well, this sucks too. I don't like big open spaces. Hard to defend if you need to. You're a pain in the ass even when you're unconscious." Henry wasn't unconscious, just immobilized, and he could hear everything McBurk was saying.

McBurk gave Henry a kick in the stomach for good measure and kept dragging him to the back of ballroom and into the dining room. Sweating and panting, McBurk dropped Henry's arms and upper torso to the floor. "Good enough," McBurk exclaimed. "Now, I'm going to look around this mausoleum of yours and see what criminal activities you're up to, Mr. Henry Jamal Steward."

Henry would have stiffened in surprise, screamed even, but he couldn't do anything except lay there, frozen on the floor. McBurk chuckled. "Oh, don't worry. I brought some dodecs to plant as evidence, so even if I don't find anything, I'll still get credit for a big drug bust. You are so screwed." He grinned, dropped a couple of sugar-cube-sized, multi-sided solids next to Henry on the floor and wandered into the drawing room, out of Henry's sight.

Laughing, McBurk continued talking to himself as his heavy footsteps made the floorboards squeal in protest. "Yeah, even Dad would have to be proud of this. Foolproof. Heh."

Dodecs. Shit. Dodecahedron was *the* most illicit of illicit drugs. Henry had never taken any, hadn't even known people who had taken any. Simple possession carried decades-long sentencing. Manufacturing it carried the death sentence. And these were just sitting there on the floor next to him.

Henry tried to move, tried to scream—anything. He could breathe and blink and that was about all. He could hear McBurk bumping around as he toured the first floor, at least a couple of rooms away.

Never before had Henry felt so helpless. He'd always been careful to have backup plans, contingencies, always something to stay one step ahead of trouble. And now this stupid, pink-skinned turd of a human being had beaten him. Had won.

It was completely illegal, of course. Not in uniform, no video or sensors. *Maybe* Henry could use that to get off on a technicality. But with heavy drug offenses, especially dodecs, the courts didn't seem to care about niceties all that much. The public applauded the hard stance against crime; so what if a couple of people were denied due process or other legal protections? Surely they had it coming anyway.

McBurk was stumbling in through the ballroom again to the dining room where Henry lay, having made an extra loud and creaking circuit around the south side of the first floor. He crossed the dining room and through the passage into the kitchen. Henry could partly see him through the doorways.

"Whooeee," McBurk exclaimed. "Well, ain't that just something? I gotta say, Henry, I have never seen anything like this. Damn. That is the hugest oven. What the hell did they cook in that?" He wandered about the massive kitchen, continuing his monologue.

"You know what?" Henry would have startled as McBurk popped into the door frame suddenly and leaned over. "I bet you could put whole bodies in that oven. People. No one would ever know. There's no sensors here, no video, no paperwork. Just some logs or some coal and—" he snapped his fingers for emphasis, "—poof. You're nothing but ash. A pile of soot. I could *end* you right here."

McBurk straightened up. "Oh, don't worry. I need you alive. I need the credit for a big dodec bust, and you and your fishy property records will give me that. You won't survive prison long enough to testify, of course, but that's not on me. Nothing anyone could prove. Heh."

He walked back into the kitchen. "But this place. Yeah, I bet I could make use of this. Buy it for a song once you're gone. Then I could really get some use out of the space." He nodded. "And the big oven."

Henry would have rolled his eyes if he could. This guy was unreal, spouting off like some cheap crime drama reality show. But he could do it, and he could get away with it. Henry tried to shout, tried to call out, but it just came out as a hushed mumble.

"Mmmghurph."

McBurk turned around to face Henry. "What was that? Oh, you like my plan, huh? Well, tell you what, fucker, after I burn a few dozen fuckers who richly deserve it, you know what I'm going do? Do you?" He walked over and leaned in close to Henry.

"Fkuu!"

"I'm going to burn this whole fucking shitshow to the ground. No evidence, and lots of insurance money. Stick that in your pen and vape it, asshole." He turned on his heel and walked back into the kitchen.

"Fkkingfkfk!" Henry screamed, shook with rage, but just a slight gurgling and more drool was all he was able to muster.

Die, die, you bastard! Henry screamed in his head. More than a scream, more than a wish, more than a prayer. Henry focused his whole being on one thought: *Die.*

Henry could see McBurk standing in the kitchen, facing the giant stove, eyes ablaze with the promise of recreational evil.

Until the floor underneath him gave way with a crash like a thunderclap.

McBurk fell straight down, his ribcage catching on the floorboards. Torso in the kitchen, legs dangling in the basement, he started screaming and flailing about.

Henry couldn't believe his luck. With McBurk trapped, maybe the effects of the neural stun would wear off, and he could take control of the situation. At least now, it was a race.

"What the fuck was that?" McBurk stopped his aimless flailing and looked genuinely terrified now.

For a moment, a very long moment, the house was completely silent. A grotesque still life of a paralyzed man on the floor watching a large pink man stuck in a hole in the floor. *Like the Wyeth painting of that girl crawling in the field.*, Henry thought, with himself playing the part of the helpless girl in the field.

The sound of ripping flesh and snapping bones shattered the silence, and McBurk screamed as if his legs had been ripped off. His torso crumpled, the blood draining quickly from his upper half into the dark of the basement.

"Fuu... *mmmmph!*" McBurk couldn't even scream. Henry couldn't really see, but it looked like McBurk's mouth was filled with powder. He was choking on it. Trying to scream, as the white ash poured out of his mouth.

Henry could do nothing but watch as McBurk's form went limp, from pasty pink to ghastly white and cyanotic blue.

The muffled screaming stopped.

Henry had plenty of time to think as he lay there, frozen on the floor. Trying to formulate a response, a plan, something. All he could do was watch as McBurk's body sagged. Blood continued draining out, and his torso settled into the floor.

I... I did that. Somehow. Or caused it. Maybe I didn't do it, but it's my fault. I killed a man. Well, more of a psychotic maggot than a man, but still... And, how? What the hell happened here?

After maybe an hour or two of watching this slow, sad, shriveling body and his own thoughts running around in circles, Henry had regained enough control to at least roll over. It took a few tries, but he managed at last, relief flowing into his numb limbs.

He hated McBurk. Would have loved to see him dead. But not here. Not like this, and not by his hand. Guilt aside, a dead cop was a magnet for more cops, brimming with bloodlust and out for revenge. It would only be a matter of time before McBurk was traced here and heavily armed troops arrived.

I've got to get rid of him. Get rid of the body. Clean up.

The words repeated themselves, chasing each other around and around in Henry's head. His arm strength came back before his legs, and he started dragging himself toward the main ballroom, aiming for the front of the house. He was able to manage a bit of a crawl, then a drunken stagger as he finally reached the front entrance.

Hello, I have half of a dead cop in my kitchen; could you lend me a hand?

Henry knew he needed help, but every variation of his plea sounded even more ridiculous than the last. He couldn't ask Enrico or Paul; even if he did, they were too far away. He needed a close neighbor, someone who would just help and not ask too many questions. Someone he could trust. Someone who really knew how to use a shovel.

Anah.

He'd help. After all, this wasn't Henry's fault.

I didn't kill McBurk. It was just an accident. The floorboards broke. Just let the cops find his body somewhere else, not here.

Henry rehearsed the line over and over as he dragged himself out to his car. McBurk's car was parked behind his. Henry startled to see that it wasn't an official police car.

Whew.

Henry almost had hope: maybe McBurk wasn't here on official business. Maybe none of the other officers knew he'd come up here. Maybe. There'd be tracking on his car, of course, but he could deal with that later. First things first.

He toppled into the driver's seat of his own car and shot down the driveway. Henry headed to his neighbor's house, rehearsing the plan in his head.

All they had to do was move the body and ditch the car somewhere, maybe pour booze all around the scene. And plant the dodecs on McBurk for good measure. Henry made a mental note to pick them up off the floor when they got back.

He turned off his headlights and running lights, and turned off the road, up the driveway past Anahat Sukhjodh Singh's sweeping gardens. Henry drove up the long driveway to the house, past the dead plants of winter. He rounded the last bend and slammed on his brakes.

The house had been destroyed.

Crumbled ruins had long been taken over by vines, trees, and brush, all now dead and gray-brown in the faint moonlight. He scrambled out of the car and wobbled in disbelief.

Wha— how—

Henry couldn't quite form the thought. The house had clearly been destroyed many years ago, probably during the war itself, or just after. And Anah? Did he come and tend the gardens out of some memory of his house, maybe his family? Maybe he lived nearby, or…

Maybe he's not even alive at all.

Henry's blood froze.

A ghost? Couldn't be. Anah was solid, speaking, as real to Henry as anyone else in town. Not some half-seen shadow or distorted reflection. But real. He whipped around, looked up and down the road, half-expecting to see him, but didn't see any sign of his friend. He slumped back into his car and slowly drove past the ruined gardens. It was hard to imagine the vibrant growth of summer. The gardens *had* been thriving and alive when Henry first arrived, hadn't they?

Suddenly, Henry wasn't sure any more. Suddenly, he wasn't sure of anything. He turned onto the main road and headed back up to Weatherly.

What. The. Fuck.

It was all he could think. Over and over.

Henry heaved open the front door and staggered into the front hall. It was all too much. All of it. He decided to head back to the kitchen to get a beer, half-a-dead body notwithstanding.

More of McBurk had sunk—or oozed—into the floorboards. Henry made a wide path around the body and rotten wood toward the refrigerator. He popped the top off a beer and took a long, cold swig.

Fuuuuck.

Somewhere in the back of his mind, he was annoyed that he couldn't be more eloquent in times of stress. Surely other people voiced whole soliloquies in their heads, while he was reduced to monosyllabic grunts and curses. But then again, how many people in the world had to face the situation where their haunted house killed a cop and ate half his body? Henry chuckled darkly.

Just you, Henry old boy, just you.

McBurk's torso slid farther into the hole, making an unwholesome squishing sound.

Oh, for fuck's sake.

Henry stormed out of the kitchen. At this rate, the body would ooze its way into the basement soon enough. He'd deal with it then. If anyone was coming after him, it wouldn't be until daylight at least. Realistically, it would be the next day. They'd notice McBurk was missing, they'd look around in the obvious places, then there'd be paperwork and the beginnings of an investigation. He had a day at least.

Actually, the sliding into the basement might be an advantage. He could clean the blood from the floorboards, maybe install some new flooring, and not worry about the chunky slime in the basement. Of course, if anyone bothered to do any DNA analysis, he was screwed… but lack of a coherent body might buy him some time.

He climbed the stairs with heavy footsteps.

Hot bath.

That's what he needed. Just take a moment. A few deep breaths. Just a short chance to relax, to gather his thoughts.

I can make this work.

He kept thinking that thought. It didn't help; things just kept getting worse. But dead cop or not, he would figure it out. He just needed a moment.

Still in a kind of a daze, he made it to the bathroom next to the master and started filling the tub with hot, soothing water. He wasn't expecting the projectile tears. The sobbing came on quickly, without warning, and he couldn't stop. Maybe the tub would fill with hot water, or maybe he'd fill it with salty tears first. It was a close call.

Tired. So tired. He moaned as he climbed into the hot water. He settled in and got comfortable, stopped sobbing and took a couple of deep breaths. It seemed to help. He took an extra deep breath and ducked his head under water for a moment.

Suddenly, he felt something holding him down, keeping his head under water. Struggling, frantic, Henry kicked and flailed in the tub. Eyes wide open, he swatted at the empty air over the tub—nothing there.

Lungs burning, desperate for oxygen, he tried to kick and use his legs for extra leverage, but nothing was working. He rolled onto his side and then face down, pressing upward with all his strength in all four limbs. The something forced him hard to the bottom of the tub, knocking the rest of the wind out of him with an explosive burst. The world began to fade, and he started to black out.

I will not die in the motherfucking bathtub!

Henry screamed in his head, and with a final last surge of strength, burst out of the water and half out of the tub, splattering hot water everywhere. Gasping and shuddering, eyes bulging, he scanned the room, but of course, there was nothing—no one—there.

"You stupid *fucking* house!" he screamed aloud. "I'm on *your* side. I'm trying to help you, dammit!"

Panting, ragged, pulse raging, he tried to be still for a moment and just listen. The house was silent except for the steady drips of water from all the drenched surfaces.

Drip.

Drip.

"For fuck's sake! I got you cleaned up. Repaired. Got rid of the squirrels in the greenhouse. Restored the old kitchen. Show a little damn gratitude! Stop trying to *fucking* kill me!"

Outside, a crow cawed. The drips echoed in the bathroom. Other than that, the house was completely silent.

Sixteen

THE FIRST HINT OF PRE-DAWN LIGHT eased through the woods. Henry grudgingly half-opened a swollen eye to consider it, paused a moment or two, then sat up from his desk in the study.

Shit. Shit, shit, shit.

He realized that just swearing to himself wasn't especially helpful. But as he shook himself awake, he felt he couldn't do much *besides* swearing to himself.

"Fuck," he said out loud. Pointless. There was no one to hear him, no one to chide him for his vulgarity or congratulate him on his edgy commentary. Just the half-crushed body of Officer McBurk back in the kitchen, dripping his entrails and fluids into the basement.

How in the name of fuck am I going to clean that up? One problem at a time. First, he had to get rid of McBurk's car.

Focus on one task. One thing at a time. That thought fortified him, gave him strength. He stood up, stretched, and tried to shake off the cobwebs. He grabbed a hand towel from the front hall bathroom, then a couple of plastic bags he remembered had been lying around in the study. Next, back to the greenhouse for a pair of gardening gloves. These were brand-new, never been used.

Perfect.

He tied the towel around his head, careful to make sure all his hair was under the towel with nothing left sticking out. The plastic bags went over his shoes. He finished up with the gardening gloves.

There. Hopefully, I won't shed any DNA in McBurk's car now.

He walked out to the car and gingerly opened the driver's door. It wasn't locked, wasn't even in sentry mode. He tapped the self-driving feature and browsed *Recent Destinations.*

— The Grumpy Yorkie (Bar/Restaurant, 1 star)

Henry punched the destination, then selected *Clear Recent Destinations.* They could still track the car here, he was sure, but no sense in making it easy. He took the dodecs that McBurk had left on the floor and slipped them under the driver's seat. Not too obvious, but easily found once someone started looking. Henry closed the door and watched as the car spun up and slid down the driveway, out of sight. It would dutifully park at the bar and wait for its owner, who would never arrive.

He pulled off the gloves and headwrap, grabbed a heavy shovel from the greenhouse and headed out to the ice house. A few commands put the equipment in stealth mode; it would be almost impossible to find without physically laying hands on it. Henry walked around the rickety boards of the ice house until he found one corner that looked especially weak. Prying with his shovel, then pushing with all his might, again and again. Pry, push. Pry, push.

Despite the rundown appearance, the ice house wasn't willing to collapse right away. Sweat ran down Henry's face, and he found himself once again panting and out of breath. He planted his feet solid on the ground, his back up against the breadth of the side wall, and pushed with all his might. Finally, with a heavy groan, the wall caved in, and with it, most of the front wall as well.

He wiped his forehead and tackled the remaining standing bits, which came down much more easily. Now the ice house was just a pile of old, rotted timbers, much like the other decrepit outbuilding ruins on the property. Anyone coming to search would have to dig through a lot of rubble to even find the stairs to the cellar. And with nothing that would show up on scans, why would they bother?

Henry sat on a timber to catch his breath. The exercise actually felt good, even at this early hour. Felt like he was accomplishing something, making progress. But it was also procrastination. He still had to face the biggest problem.

The body. How in hell do I get that out of the floorboards?

Rope. He wasn't exactly sure how, but somehow, he'd need rope. Rudder's opened early, serving something similar to coffeesynth but more corrosive. Henry went upstairs and changed his clothes, then headed down into town.

There were no other customers at the store, and no Earl Rudder dispensing barbs, just a sleepy young kid behind the counter who couldn't care less that Henry was buying a large coil of rope at 7:30 in the morning. Henry grunted in lieu of small talk and hurried back up to Weatherly.

There, in the ruined fields in front of the wreckage of Anah's house, was Anah himself. Poking at the dirt with a hoe, or shovel. Henry stopped the car, unsure of what he was seeing—unsure of what was real. Was that really Anah? Was he a ghost? Or just a sad old man who couldn't let go of his hideous tragedy?

Henry got out.

"Hey, Anah," he called softly.

Anah looked up from the dirt, infinite sadness in his eyes. "You've seen the house, then?"

Henry nodded.

Anah looked up the driveway. "I lost them all. My wife, my daughters… Killed. And for what? What good did that do anyone?"

Henry paused a minute, finally summoning up an extra ounce of courage. "Are you a ghost? You don't look like a ghost. You look… solid. Real."

Anah threw his head back and laughed; a hollow, macabre sound. "A what? A ghost now, you say. And would you know what a ghost looks like? How do you know I do not look like a ghost if you have never seen a ghost before?"

Henry sputtered, started to reply, but Anah continued.

"I had a friend once, who wanted to visit United China. As he was leaving, another friend of mine said, 'Oh, if you're going to China, be sure to say hello to my dear friend Xi Lao there.' We laughed, because of course, China is an immense country. He would never just 'run into' his friend."

Henry's look of confusion spread. Anah turned to face him fully. "Let me ask you this. Do you think all people in China are all alike? Or people in New Chicago, or the Republic of California? No? Then why would you think all ghosts are alike? Some are helpful. Some are sad. Some are simply destruction itself. Surely no two alike." He turned back and began poking at the dirt again.

Henry didn't know what to say. Or do. He stammered a question. "Why are you here?"

"I still have work to do, of course."

"Are you real? Are you even *actually* here?"

Anah looked up and smiled peacefully. "Are you?"

Tears welled in Henry's eyes; he was just overcome with it all. He looked back at his car, maybe to reassure himself that it was real, solid. He turned back to face Anah, but he had disappeared.

Henry was alone in the ruined gardens.

Head swimming, Henry walked slowly back to his car.

Was he ever even really there? Did I imagine the whole thing?

Am I going crazy?

He stood there a long minute, then shook his head. This was just another mystery that would have to wait. First things first—he had a body to dispose of.

The car crunched over the gravel of the driveway, and Henry tried to focus on the task at hand. He had to extricate the body from the shattered floorboards first, then figure out how to get rid of it. Acid? Fire? Burial?

He didn't have any acid, fire would produce a lot of smoke that might be noticed, and burial would not stand up to scrutiny of dogs or sensors. He shook his head as he made his way through the house to the kitchen. He'd think of something. Get the body up and out first, then figure out what to do with it. Maybe cut it up?

Henry was mulling over his choices as he turned the corner into the kitchen.

The body was gone.

Oh, you've got to be fucking kidding me. Now what?

Slowly, he crept up to the hole in the floor. Only, it wasn't a hole. The boards were ripped up and broken but were just lying there flat. There was no gaping hole, no access to the basement. No blood, and no body.

He poked his toe at one of the boards, then gingerly put his full weight on it. Nothing. Despite the damage, the floor remained solid. He set the rope down on a side table and left the kitchen.

Doesn't make sense. None of this makes sense.

Had he imagined it? Was McBurk even here?

Of course, he was. You saw it. His car was here. Something killed him, and now the body is completely gone.

On the one hand, this solved a problem for Henry—he wouldn't have to struggle with hiding a body if there was no body to hide.

But where did it go?

And more importantly, could it come back?

The logical thing, of course, was to check the basement. Henry couldn't face that, not alone. Maybe with Enrico and Paul and enough light to get a suntan again. He'd have to think of some excuse to get them back, and quickly.

"Oh, fuck it," he said aloud, grabbed an LED disc, and yanked open the basement stairs anyway.

The near part of the kitchen was just off the staircase, in theory, Henry could look over that way without actually leaving the staircase itself. He turned on the basement lights and went down the stairs slowly, keeping a firm hand on the new railing. At the bottom, he shone the LED over to what should have been the underside of the kitchen area.

Unbroken ceiling.

There was nothing at all. Nothing indicating that half a body and torn-up flooring had crashed through here.

Was it actually here? And then, an even more chilling thought. Something Anah had said.

Am I?

"Yeah, just some broken floorboards. Guess they'd been sealed up in that old kitchen for a long time. Thanks."

Henry hung up the call with Enrico and took a swig of hot coffeesynth. He'd get the flooring fixed today and head down to the library at his usual time.

Best to carry on as usual. Nothing to see here.

He continued getting ready and drove down into town. As Henry drove onto the main road, he noticed that Anah was nowhere to be found; his ruined gardens lay cold and fallow in the dead of winter.

It was his turn to open the library for the day. Henry unlocked the modern glass doors and threw on the main lights. He spent the morning cataloging and shelving some new arrivals: spy thrillers, romance novels, some government gibberish, propaganda for the children, the usual assortment. It was an effort not to run screaming down the polished floors in the main hallway.

What if the station knows that McBurk was last seen at Weatherly?

That was the question.

McBurk was just enough of an egomaniacal shit that he could have come after me without paperwork, without auth.

Henry kept telling himself that it was *probably* off the record. Sometime today, the cops would find McBurk's car down at the bar and figure he'd wandered off somewhere blind drunk.

Not too far from the truth.

Henry dusted, cleaned, helped a few library patrons looking for various best-sellers, and tried not to panic. Esmeralda joined him after lunch, just before a scheduled field trip from a batch of school kids.

"Afternoon, J," she said as she hung up her coat and such.

"Hey," Henry replied, with a subtle shift in his tone that Esmeralda picked up on immediately.

She shot him a look. "Well, what is it now? What rabbit hole are you halfway down already; what thread are you tugging on that ought not be tugged?"

Henry snorted. Not quite a laugh, certainly not a laugh-out-loud, just an expulsion of humorous air.

"Up near Weatherly," he launched right in with no preamble. "There's an old estate right off the main road. Fellow named Anahat Singh. What do you know about it?"

Esmeralda winced, took a deep breath. "Sad story. His wife had a doctorate, PhD in biogenetics or something. One of the factions wanted to enlist her for the war, some sort of bioweapon." She shuddered. "Anyway, she refused to help. They killed the entire family and burned the estate to the ground."

Henry gulped. "The… entire family? Anahat too?"

"Yes." Esmeralda shook her head. "Anahat, his wife, his children, I think his mother-in-law, perhaps a few other relatives. Then they burned it all to the ground to cover up the evidence. And send a message, I suppose. Not that it mattered, the war ended anyway not long after. Such a waste. Terrible waste." She turned away.

Henry didn't know what to say. Or think. He'd *talked* with Anah, multiple times, watched him till and poke at his fabulous gardens. Hadn't he?

"How do you know Anahat and his family?" Esmeralda asked, suddenly curious. "That was all many years ago."

Henry felt like his entire world caved in on him. A fractal sinkhole, folding in on itself, swallowing him, enveloping him. "I… I…" He couldn't quite form the words.

Esmeralda waited patiently and did not prompt or interrupt.

Henry swallowed hard, looked up at the coffered ceiling, down at the floor, added several other gyrations, and finally admitted, "I met Anah. Talked to him. He was…" Henry choked up, tears welling in his eyes. "He was my friend."

Esmeralda looked up sharply. "What? That's not possible. He's been dead for… his whole family… how…" She trailed off in stunned silence.

Henry rocked back. "I don't know. I just… I don't know. But I talked to him, every couple of days at least, right there, by the side of the road. In front of his house, in his gardens. Well, what used to be his gardens. I mean…"

They sat together in silence for a long while. An old man came in, rummaged in the stacks a bit, and came back with a book on sailing. Esmeralda checked him out and mumbled a few courteous words.

The front door closed with solid thud, and Henry offered, "I talked to Anah… regularly. He wasn't a ghost or anything. He was right there, damn it! Solid! Real. A…" He choked up again. "A real nice guy. Down to earth. Not judgmental."

Esmeralda sighed. "I didn't know him well, but I'd met him a few times around town. His wife was out of town a lot, off to conferences, meetings. I wondered why they had settled out here. Seemed to me that maybe she belonged in the megapolis. Researching, curing disease, that sort of thing. But, J, they all died. Years ago. Long before you got here. I don't know what you saw." She took a deep breath. "But I tell you, Anah has been dead for a long time."

They both just kind of sat there for the rest of the day, numbly acknowledging the passage of time. A handful of patrons came and went, the sun grudgingly rose and hurriedly set. Henry drove back to Weatherly. The moon was bright. Somehow, in the winter time, the moon always seemed extra bright and melancholy, casting sharp shadows on the barren landscape.

He cast a sideways glance at Anah's estate off the main road as he drove by, but it remained cold and dead. As it had been. As it should have been.

The house at Weatherly was cold and dark. Henry turned on lights as he made his way from the entry hall back to the kitchen, but it felt futile. Such little light against an infinite void of darkness. His dream of rural fresh vegetables hadn't worked out, at least not yet, so he microwaved a small, pre-packaged meal. It was bland and unsatisfying. No surprise there.

He was absently tapping his fork against the package when he heard loud knocking at the door.

Probably Enrico and Paul, he grumbled as he abandoned his pathetic meal and wandered back out to the front of the house to answer the door.

Two men in armored business suits stood there.

"Henry Jamal Steward?" the first one asked.

Fuck. Fuuuuuuuuck, was all that Henry could think.

"Yeah," he admitted in a small, weak voice.

"May we come in?" the larger one asked, as he and his partner pushed past Henry into the hallway.

Once they were inside, Henry reluctantly closed the door.

The first one turned to him and announced, "I am Agent Silver. This is Agent Green."

Henry nodded but didn't say anything.

"We are following up on an investigation by an Officer McBurk into drug production in this area. Do you know anything about that?"

Henry swallowed hard, his face white, his soul wanting to flee his body and run into the dark of the night. With huge effort, he calmed his voice and said quietly but steadily, "I've met McBurk a couple of times, down at the bar. But never in any official capacity. I don't think he likes me." Henry almost said *liked* me, in past tense, but caught himself just in time.

Agent Green had walked down the entrance hall and just into the ballroom. Silver motioned Henry to follow. "Why do you think McBurk doesn't like you?"

Henry shrugged. "I'm new in town. Got a job to oversee repairs and restoration here at Weatherly. I don't really know anything about the history here or anything. I'm not really used to living out here, you know, it's not like back in the megapolis. So, lots of things he could take offense at, I suppose."

"This is a really big house," Agent Green commented as he wandered through the small lobby by the bathroom and into the study at the front of the house. His eyes scanned the large windows and the door on the other side of the room. He headed for it.

Agent Silver kept talking as they followed. "Did McBurk mention anything about a dodec lab?"

"No. Not to me, anyway. Last time I saw him at the bar, he did seem pretty angry at something though. But maybe he's just one of those guys who always gets angry when he drinks." Henry's face would have passed any biometric exam, and probably was doing exactly that right now. He was telling the truth.

Silver smiled slightly. "And when was that? At the bar?"

Henry shrugged again. "Couple of nights ago, I guess."

Green opened the door to the private library, noted the small, non-opening windows, and grunted. So quickly that Henry didn't even have time to react, Silver shoved him through the doorway into the small library, closed and locked the door, taking the large, old-fashioned key with him.

Silver called out through the locked door, "Now you just wait right there, Mr. Steward, while we have a good long look around." Silver and Green both chuckled and headed back out through the ballroom.

"Man, I haven't been up this way in *years*," Green was saying as their voices faded from earshot. "We used to use the place a lot back when..."

Henry couldn't hear the rest.

Seventeen

HENRY RATTLED THE DOORKNOB, just to make sure
they really had locked it. And taken the key. He was
trapped in the private library off the study.

For the love of fuck… Henry started, then stopped.
He had run out of swears, run out of disbelief, run out
of belief itself. He just felt numb.

And trapped.

What if they found McBurk's body? What if they
found the dodecs that McBurk had tried to plant as evidence? Henry thought he'd hidden them well enough,
but…

Henry sat heavily and hung his head, only a breath
away from sobbing uncontrollably.

*I've got two armored agents wandering free in my
house.*

And these weren't local morons. These were high-
end agents, probably from Central. Trained, armed, and

live streaming with sensors, facial and spatial recognition; everything.

Not that that mattered now. They knew his name.

How the fuck? Henry wailed silently. *How did they find me?* His hands were trembling; he sat on them. He had to get out of here. Now. All the oddities with the house, his struggles to live outside the comforts of the megapolis, none of that mattered now.

They were going to kill him. He knew that. It was just a matter of time. Lock him here in the library for a while, torture him, perhaps. Kill him, definitely. If only he could magically disappear.

Disappear. Magically. Like Ferguson. The old man who "magically" appeared in the upstairs guest bedroom without being seen.

A secret fucking passage. Hell yeah! Henry jumped up. He'd forgotten to look for it, what with all the rest of this hell going on. Now was as good a time as any. He looked closely at the floor, trying to see any obvious marks from a door that swept in. It only took a few minutes, but he made a full sweep around the small room.

One thing at a time. Focus on one thing.

Next, he looked at the floor molding, where the wall or bookcases met the floor. Surely there would be a joint or something. But another full pass around the room and there was nothing he could see, nothing that suggested a concealed door.

He started a second pass to look again when one of the common, giant wind gusts buffeted the house. The house shook and shuddered, and Henry felt the subtlest breath of wind near his face.

A draft.

He froze and moved toward the wall where he'd been standing. He was on the corner near the front of the house. He frowned. Of course, this had to be it. From the outside of the house, there was a turret on this corner. But here, in the small private library, there was only an angled wall on that corner with a built-in bookcase. All the walls were lined with bookcases, and this one seemed to fit in smoothly with its neighbors.

But there must be a staircase behind here somehow. There was room for it, and weren't hidden passages always behind bookcases? Seemed an obvious choice.

Henry pushed, pulled, and bothered every ornamental carving he could find, but nothing budged. The shelves were long emptied of books, and the shelves themselves seemed very plain. There were several small drawers under the shelves at waist height, but these were empty, too. Henry tried to pull them all the way out, to see if there was a mechanism or button hidden behind, but they were held captive by design. He slammed the middle drawer shut in frustration and braced himself against the bookshelf.

He pushed with all his might. Nothing.

Fuck you, house.

He pulled back and stormed around the room a few times. The desk was just a regular desk; it wasn't built-in or connected to the floor—he'd moved it a few feet in various directions over the last weeks. Unlikely there was any kind of release lever there.

The only thing that moved anywhere near the bookcase were the drawers. Two small drawers flanking a larger centered drawer. Henry paused and considered them. He opened the small drawer on the left side first and looked closely at the interior.

The inside of the top of the drawer was worn smooth. He closed it and opened the middle drawer. It didn't seem to have any wear patterns. Next, the small drawer on the far right. It was worn smooth on the top as well.

Hmmmm.

Henry made sure all three drawers were closed fully, then opened the two small drawers together and pulled hard—not using the knobs, which looked dainty, but with his hands cupped over the top lip of the drawer face. Right where the wear patterns were.

As he pulled hard, he felt a click, and the whole bookcase eased back into the space behind. He pushed on the bookcase, and it gently opened as if it were a door, quietly creaking.

Sonofabitch. A secret fucking staircase. For real.

It was pitch black in the little room, so Henry grabbed an LED disk that was lying on the table and walked through the bookcase-doorway.

The turret was small, cramped. Henry noted a heavy iron bar that acted as a latch to keep the bookcase-door closed. The staircase was made of stone, circular, built into the outside wall of the turret and spiraling up to the next floor. There was no handrail.

Anyone running into this staircase from upstairs would just fall and die. Henry wondered if that had been a deliberate security measure or just the callous construction ethic of the day. He took a deep breath, which didn't really help his trembling hands and shaking legs, and mounted the staircase, quietly closing the bookcase-door behind him.

Slowly, carefully, silently, trying to stay near the outer wall, he climbed the circular stairs up to the second floor. By the light of the LED, he saw another iron bar across the doorway in front of him. He lifted and pulled, and the wall section opened toward him. He walked through and found himself in the dressing room of the large guest bedroom at the front of the house.

You horny bastard, Ferguson. Henry grinned. Great way to "check in" on the guests.

Well, you've saved my ass today, and I thank you for that!

Then Henry realized that he didn't really have a plan. Yes, he'd escaped the small private library and was free, but he was still trapped in the house with two roving—and armed—agents.

He could get to the servants' staircase from here, through the little lobby between the guest bedroom and the balcony over the ballroom. From there, he could get to the first floor again, but he'd have to cross the ballroom to get to the front entrance hall and door.

That's a big, exposed area.

Alternatively, he could go all the way down to the basement and try and get out through the coal chute.

Great, if the fucking cops don't kill me, the fucking house will.

He sat on the edge of the moldy guest bed, waiting for a better idea. Faintly, somewhere in the house, he could hear their footsteps and voices.

Laughing.

His mind raced. There weren't really any exits on this side of the house. The greenhouse, the patio off the breakfast room—those were all on the other side of the house from here. The dining room exited to the rear, but he really needed a front exit.

Why?

His car was out front. So, obviously, he had to exit to the front of the house. But there was no way to get to the front door without crossing the ballroom, where he'd surely be seen. Unless… the servants' staircase. He could make it down to the basement and clamber out the coal chute. There was a chance he could make it out to the car undetected.

And then what? Well, that was the real problem. They knew his name. They knew he was here and could trace any routes out of town easily. Where would he go? How could he escape this?

Henry hung his head in his hands as he realized he couldn't. They'd find him. They'd kill him. His only chance now was maybe in the Wastelands, scavenging his existence, hiding in holes away from the sensors and scans.

He stood up and patted the caked dust from the bed off of his pants.

Fuck it. If that's how it is, then that's how it is. Weatherly Hall as an escape was a great idea. Didn't work out. Fuck it. Off to the Wastelands it is. Still better than being tortured and killed here by these miserable pieces of shit.

With grim determination, he stepped quietly from the guest bedroom into the small lobby. The door on the far side opened onto the servants' staircase. Gently, he eased the door opened. It groaned, but only a little, and he was flying down the narrow servants' stairs as quick as a shadow.

Henry had never felt *relief* in the basement before; this was a first. The LED disk was woefully inadequate for the yawning chasm of inky black, but it was enough. He crossed the short axis of the house to the coal chute, which was at the front right corner of the house as you looked at it from the driveway.

The coal chute, of course, was designed for shoveling coal from the driveway into the basement, ultimately to be carried over to the undercroft of the kitchen. It was certainly not designed to be climbed. The sides were smoothed brick; there were no handholds or steps or anything. Henry sighed. The chute was small enough that he could press against both sides at once and hold himself in position with his hands or his feet. So, crablike, grunting, he pushed himself up the chute.

He tried to be quiet about it, but there were a few more bumps and scrapes than he would have liked. Finally, he made it up to the door, a warped, rusted metal beast. As slowly as he could, he eased the bolt back and softly opened the door into the cold, black night.

He tumbled up and over the lip, straightened up, and breathed a sigh of relief.

It might have been a wooden bat, or a metal bar, or maybe just flesh and bone, but whatever hit him in the head hit him really hard. His knees buckled, air rushed out of his chest, and just as he was losing consciousness, he heard the words, "Going somewhere?"

—————————————

It wasn't that Henry saw black, exactly. It was more of a dark, dull red. He was vaguely aware of being carried, or dragged. He felt numb all over and couldn't even form a solid thought. Sharp pain as they dropped him to the floor. Where was he? Face down on the floor, somewhere in the house. A loud, creaking, groaning noise tried to get his attention. Maybe it was important? Then voices, muffled and indistinct.

"Let's fire it up; he's going in!"

Dragged again, a face full of something soft and powdery, and the slam of an enormous door almost brought Henry to consciousness. The dark red haze was pounding in his head in time with his pulse.

"Hey, check out the pile of cardboard. We can use that," said a muffled voice.

"What about your carbon license?" the other voice laughed, followed by clanging and shuffling noises.

With a start, Henry jerked his head up and realized where he was. They had thrown him inside the big oven in the kitchen and were loading it up with cardboard to burn.

They were going to burn him alive. No judge, no jury, no paperwork. He flailed himself over to the heavy cast-iron door and shook it, kicked against it. Locked from the outside.

Trapped.

Henry's heart was pounding so hard he was sure he was breaking his own ribs. His arms and legs were trembling uncontrollably. He couldn't have turned a doorknob even if there was one, and his jaw was clenched in a tight spasm. He couldn't even scream, not on the outside. But on the inside, he was screaming in pure, blind terror.

Then something snapped.

All the years of looking over his shoulder, all the fears real and imagined: fear of his father, his classmates, neighbors who might turn him in, the government itself… all came crashing down at once. What was he most afraid of? Pain. Death. And now all of that was upon him in an instant. He would die here, in searing, indescribable pain. And with that realization, suddenly he could *see*.

The figures weren't ghosts, not like in the movies. He could see them—feel them. But they weren't there. It was like part of his brain saw them and part didn't. He could make them come and go, like closing one eye and then the other. Two different places, in the same place, all at once.

They were hunched over in the oven, with him, clothed in pain. He saw children, young kids, their charred, blacked bones poking out of bodies caked with ash. Their faces were hollow, empty—no eyes, no teeth. Just ruined skin draped over empty skulls.

Dimly, in the part of his brain that wasn't shrieking in horror, Henry remembered Fiona's theory that the resistance leaders were brought to Weatherly, tortured, and killed. He realized in that moment that they weren't killed here.

Their children were.

The notion came to him as clear as day. The kids of politicians and business leaders were kidnapped, brought here, tortured and killed. And now, he would join them in some kind of fiery hell. Henry uselessly kicked at the door. It ignored him.

More muffled voices. He couldn't tell who was who.

"That's a lot of kindling, but we need some wood or coal or compressed firelogs or something."

"There's a lot of wood here in the kitchen—shelving, cabinet doors. Let's rip that down and throw it in."

Muffled tearing, shrieking sounds of splintered wood, banging and more. It sounded like they were tearing up the kitchen.

Henry strained to see anything in the darkness—other than the ghostly, burned bodies that floated around him. He tried to ignore the apparitions and felt around for another door, a hatch, a flue, anything.

A sudden roar of noise and a blast of heat came up from the iron floor. They had lit the stove. It started getting hot—fast. Henry pounded his sweating fists against the unyielding iron, screaming on the inside and the outside now. He was just one long scream, a futile and small noise against the swift roar of the fire.

He looked around in a black panic, then took a deep breath of the scalding air and saw the figures again. They were motioning to him. He didn't know what it meant.

They can see me. That was different, maybe, from the other apparitions and incidents he'd had at Weatherly. If they could see him, then…

With a sharp shock, he thought back to that night where he dreamed that *he* was the ghost wandering through the walls of an earlier Weatherly.

If it was a dream…

A figure next to him waved the charred stump of its hand, motioning Henry to the door. Henry understood.

Maybe. What the hell, it's worth a try.

Henry closed his eyes—not that he could see anything in the dark of the oven anyway—and thought back to that night. Back to the feeling of wandering the house as a ghost. The grim, burned figures nodded excitedly and became more solid, more detailed.

That night. That dream. It had felt so… different. He couldn't explain it, couldn't put it into words. But he tried hard to feel that way again, to recreate that strange sensation.

In a few moments, the figures became more real, and the oven became ghostly. The thing closest to him turned its empty eye sockets to the oven door and waved to it. Henry glided over, legs outstretched, and slid into the kitchen.

The agents wavered and shimmered as ghosts in the kitchen, laughing and feeding the fire. Henry shifted his thinking, as when waking from a dream, and the men solidified. He grabbed the nearest one and dragged him into shadow, hurling him toward the oven. The second agent lurched after them in shock and surprise, right past Henry. Henry kicked him hard in the ass, and the momentum carried him through the ghostly oven door.

Adjusting his thoughts again, Henry shifted, and was solid, real, and in the kitchen. One agent was trapped completely in the oven, roaring flames licking the white-hot iron, almost drowned out by his screaming.

But the second agent hadn't made it all the way in. When he shifted back into the oven, only one leg and part of one arm was caught inside, as the rest of him scrambled back into the kitchen.

"My fucking leg!" He shrieked in horror and pain as he pulled the seared stump of his leg from the oven door. Writhing in pain on the floor for only a moment, he grabbed for his sidearm with his one good arm.

Henry flung himself out of the kitchen and through the doorway. He tried to shift his thoughts again; tried to recapture that strange feeling.

Nothing happened.

Just then a small explosion ripped through the door frame, spraying flaming shards of wood and metal everywhere.

"I'll fucking kill you! You motherfucking sonofa bitch! Fuck you!" Another explosion as the agent fired off a round. He was scrambling to get out of the kitchen, crawling, dragging his ruined body as best he could, howling in pain and bestial rage.

Henry dodged through the passageway into the stairwell for the servants' staircase. He felt a sharp pang as he bolted up the stairs, grabbed his side, and saw blood on his hand.

Fuck me, must have caught some debris. He kept running up the stairs, ignoring the burning pain in his side, up to the balcony. From there, he ran to the small stairs leading up to the attics.

Try climbing stairs without your leg, bastard. Henry panted as got to the attic level. Out the windows, he'd seen a drone above the agents' patrol car, hovering in sentry mode. Henry hoped that the heat from the fire drowned out any heat-signature details, for now, at least. But he'd need to specifically jam that drone.

Can't let him get to the car and call for help.

Henry pulled out a burner phone. He scrambled his card ID and sent a text, from one random number to some other random, unknowing number: *Hey Joe; I'm running late.* The receiver would think it was a wrong number or a butt-dial. But Henry's drone shield would have scanned the message, recognized the code phrase, and activated the next-level comms blocker.

That will buy me at least a little time.

Henry tried again to shift. He closed his eyes and tried to recreate that state of mind. Still nothing.

"Fucker! I'm going to get you!" Another explosion ripped the staircase somewhere as the agent shot wildly, hoping for a hit. Henry huffed himself down the rest of the long, windowless, central hall until he saw the locked door with the ornate brass keyplate.

Never did find that key. Well, neither will that turd-nozzle. Henry stood in front of the door and took a deep breath, trying as hard as he could to recreate that strange feeling. This time it worked. He shifted, turning the door into a wavering, watery vision. He walked through and shifted back.

Officer Reynolds glanced over at the monitor, annoyance clear on her face.

PACKET LOSS EXCEEDS ALARM THRESH-OLD. LOST COMMUNICATIONS LINK.

She scrolled back in the log. Nothing remarkable. It was the two agents up at Weatherly, there to conduct an interview. Nothing in the drone feed indicated any sort of problem, just increasing packet loss then no communications at all. She punched a button.

"Lieutenant Tabor, we may have a problem." Tabor's image came up on the screen, and she explained the loss of the drone feed.

"They were up there asking after McBurk?" Tabor asked.

"Yes, sir."

He scrolled back through the drone footage himself. "I don't see anything. Certainly nothing to worry about. Dumbass McBurk wanders off, dead drunk somewhere, and Central sends out a couple of goons to look into it. Now there's weak comms out at the ass-end of the mesh. So what." Tabor rubbed his temples. "It doesn't matter.

When those two morons check in, tell them they need to get back to Central ASAP."

"Why, what's up?" Reynolds asked.

"Haven't you seen the main feed?" Tabor asked. "Some nutball is tossing grenades off the roof of a skyscraper down onto people. Milspec grenades, at that—not the weenie home defense kind. He's blowing holes through the roadways and taking out chunks of neighboring buildings. It's a real shitshow."

Reynolds blanched. "Why haven't they taken him out yet? They have armed drones—"

"He's wearing even more explosives. If they miss, they might take out the whole building, or a good chunk of it. They've sent for an HD sharp-shooter drone, so I'm thinking they'll nail him shortly. But they are recalling all available personnel for crowd control and shit. Lordy, what a mess." Tabor shook his head. "Meanwhile, be thankful we are up here, far away from it all. And fuck McBurk. He'll turn up begging for his job back, and I'm not going to grant it this time. He is so fucking fired."

Tabor clicked and terminated the call.

Reynolds reset the alarm and turned off the monitoring channel, then brought up the main feed to follow the live feed of the grenade tosser.

Eighteen

It had been a couple of years ago. Henry had gotten permits and nav data for a trip south to the Midlands. Officially, it was a supposed to be a month-long vacation.

But in fact, he was going to meet someone. Someone who claimed to have a full, unedited dump of pre-war Wikipedia—with all the original countries, all the original truths before that had become a dirty word. He was loaded with blank memory crystals for the dump and a collection of his own for trade.

He was very proud of his collection, which he'd gathered and traded for over the years. He had a full, uncensored version of the Gutenberg library, digitizations of the old masters from Da Vinci to Rubens, later impressionists including all of Monet, Cézanne, Cassatt, and others. A full King James Bible. Recipes, how to grow your own food, a lot of off-the-grid stuff. A treasure trove of independent Western civilization. Downloaded since the earliest BBS days of FIDOnet and Usenet, and the pre-surveillance days of the internet.

Most all of which was now either re-copyrighted, censored, or just plain outlawed.

After the war, it become all-too-obvious that the net was ever-changing. No one kept paper records any more. Everything was online, and minor facts kept changing. Sometimes even major facts. Maybe you remembered it differently. Was that your own faulty memory, or had the official records been altered? It got harder and harder to tell. Data—and people—could just disappear. Copyright laws got insanely complicated, and re-copyright made it just about impossible to ever own your own copy of anything.

But all the time he amassed his collection, Henry had hoped someday to escape. To slip off quietly to one of the few remaining remote areas. Not just a small town, or a farming town, but one that was truly "off-the-grid" and away from it all. His meeting to trade for a full copy of Wikipedia was the jewel, the gemstone at the center of his plans.

But as he was crossing into Midlands, he was randomly selected for a full, intensive border search. They found the memory crystals he was carrying and all the cash. He'd hidden them in the lining of his luggage, shielded from sensors, but the agents had ripped his luggage apart with knives. So primitive. But effective.

They seized it all, and Henry was jailed for a month, then placed on a watch list.

He'd been a model citizen in the years since then—as far as any official records and surveillance could tell. In truth, he'd gotten all the data he wanted and much more, eventually. It ended up being much more expensive than his first contact in the Midlands had offered, but it was all via dead drops. Much safer, and he was never caught.

But as he collected more and more data troves, there was a problem. It didn't all align. Much of it was contradictory; there were multiple versions that claimed to be original and unaltered, which clearly weren't original and had been altered. His long search for truth had been futile, and many basic facts of history remained unanswered.

And in the course of his collection, he'd gotten into data and tech that carried severe penalties. Much worse than a month in the Midland's prisons overlooking the Chesapeake Bay.

But on top of all that, worse than the watch list and the contraband, was a dead Officer Eric McBurk and one dead high-level state agent. Screaming his last breaths on this earth, locked in the oven that had killed so many already. And one not-yet dead state agent, shrieking like a banshee, firing explosive bolts as he dragged his burned and dismembered body up the stairs to find Henry.

Henry sighed.

Well, the house and I killed two of these maggots, what's one more?

He felt somewhat safe and protected behind the locked door. The agent wouldn't be able to unlock it. But hearing another blast, Henry realized with a sinking feeling that the wooden door, no matter how solid and sturdy it was, wouldn't stop the agent from blasting his way through.

Henry looked around in the dim light of the attic room. Much more ornate, fancier furniture than in the other attic storeroom he'd seen. Dusty but obviously once highly-polished mahogany, gilt picture frames, and small chests. Idly, he opened the nearest.

No fucking way. Guess I was wrong about the family silver not being included.

It may or may not have been the original family's silver, but it was old, and there was a lot of it. Large serving dishes, plates, punch bowls—everything you'd need for a *large* party.

Henry vowed then and there to do just that.

If I get out of this, I'll make this house fucking party central. No more hiding. Bring it.

Slam. Bang. Doors and explosions. Thuds, and a damp dragging sound. The agent was working his way down the hallway toward Henry.

Shit. Henry abruptly stopped daydreaming about rich, ornate parties in the house and tried to focus on the immediate threat.

He's getting closer.

The creaking floors would have been enough to betray the agent's progress, but he was beyond any care or caution. Henry could hear the sickening thud, slide, thud, slide as the agent dragged himself through the house, firing with wild abandon as he went.

Henry looked around, frantically now, for something to use as a weapon or a shield. He grabbed a large silver serving plate. It was better than nothing, but he didn't think it would stop an explosive bolt.

The crashing noises got closer and closer, then quickly stopped.

Fuuuck… Henry panicked as he realized the agent was probably right outside the locked door. He tried to shift his thinking again, tried to visualize the agent outside the door. In his mind's eye, he saw him lifting his pistol and bracing himself to fire on the door.

Henry took a deep breath and tried to concentrate. He pictured the agent wavering, turning watery. He pictured him sinking, floating gently down through the floors back to the kitchen—they should be right over the oven from here.

The agent screamed as he materialized downstairs.

Henry unlocked the door and ran into the hallway, down the stairs toward the kitchen. A blast nearly got him in the face as he was brought up short at the foot of the servants' stairs.

Missed! Fuck!

The agent was not in the oven but was hurling himself out of the kitchen again toward Henry, bellowing like a wounded and desperate animal.

Henry pictured him again, then pictured the floor underneath him. He imagined the floor turning all ghostly and full of mist. The agent's low bellowing suddenly switched to a high-pitched scream, then fell silent.

Cautiously, Henry crept toward the kitchen and poked his head around the corner. Hot, stinking of burning flesh, but empty. He'd sent him to the basement.

Slowly, carefully, Henry opened the basement door and walked down. There was no screaming, no sound at all. It was quiet. Not a peaceful, relaxed quiet, but the quiet of the end; of finality. Despite the dark and gloom, Henry could see the tableau unfold before him.

There was the agent, floating in mid-air.

Henry started, despite himself, and blinked hard. He got closer and realized that no, the agent wasn't floating. He was hanging by the meat hooks on the wall of a store-room. The hooks protruded from his shattered chest, blood running out and down the drain in the floor. The agent's gun was on the floor, and Henry bent over and took it.

The agent gurgled, whimpered, then fell completely silent. Just the slow drop of his blood, and his life, running out. But then he was hanging again, the hook bursting through his chest. Hanging, suffering, bleeding out, dying. All at once; over and over again.

Like a barber pole illusion.

He climbed the stairs slowly back up to the kitchen and left the basement to its business.

Henry sighed but didn't curse, even to himself. He didn't yell; he didn't sob. He just sighed. With the help of the dead, or maybe the house itself, he'd killed them. All of them.

The state would find out soon enough, and then they'd send full, armored squads in hypercars. There was no way he could take them all on. They'd blow up the whole house with him in it; he'd never even have a chance to fight them. Hell, it was possible they'd target him from an orbital platform. Strictly speaking, that sort of thing was illegal and against international treaty. But that hadn't stopped it from happening during the war and hadn't stopped it since. His illegal memory crystals were the least of his problems now.

The heat from the oven was still so intense that the whole of the kitchen felt like a resort sauna. Except for the smell. The stench of burnt flesh was one of those things that stayed with you, stuck in your nostrils. Hard to get out, hard to forget.

Henry wandered aimlessly through the house from there and ended up in the bathroom upstairs, drawing himself a bath. Maybe a nice hot bath would soothe his aching muscles and help get the fume of roasted agents out of his nose.

The pipes squealed and groaned like demons from the depths, the hot water steamed, and Henry climbed into the tub. He had *just* gotten comfortable when invisible hands once again crushed him under the water, trying to hold him down.

Henry didn't struggle, didn't scream. He waited a moment, then lifted his head to take a breath and rolled over onto his stomach. The pressure stopped for a moment, as if in confusion. Henry lifted his head and yelled, "Alright, if you're here, you can give me a damn backrub."

There was silence for a few heartbeats. Then the invisible hand pressure was back, rolling on Henry's back.

I do not fucking believe it, he thought to himself. After a few minutes of massage, the hands—and whatever they were attached to—went away. Henry rolled over onto his back.

Well, now.

Henry finished his bath in peace, dressed, and went back to the kitchen. The fire had died down but wasn't out yet.

That might be a while.

Using a stick of wood from the ruined cabinets, he opened the heavy oven door. There wasn't much left of the agent. A few bits of bone, maybe. Hard to tell. It was still hot in the kitchen. He wandered out to the front of the house.

The agents' car was still there. Surely the comms failure had been noticed by now, to say nothing of the fact that the agents hadn't reported in.

Either way, there's going to be a lot of armed people here pretty quickly.

But somehow, that didn't worry Henry. Things were different now. He couldn't explain it. He didn't control the house or anything, or command the ghostly presences. But he felt they understood that he was on their side—he wasn't the state; he wasn't the enemy.

He started back toward the house, but then had an idea. He walked back to the agents' car and sent a text to a randomly-selected phone number:

Thanks for the flowers.

The anti-drone gear picked up the text and sent a flood of messages to any hardware on the property. In a few seconds, the locks on the car popped. Henry opened the passenger's side door and tossed the remaining dodecs in on the seat, and locked it behind him.

Henry walked back in through the heavy front door and closed it gently behind him. He glanced down out of habit and saw that the ash piles still had not returned.

He looked up again, and adjusting his thinking slightly, saw the man in the butler's clothing. Pale, slick-backed hair. He nodded at Henry.

Henry smiled and nodded back.

Nineteen

It wasn't yet dawn when Henry got the alarm about the drones. More than a dozen, military grade, ringing the house.

Mechanized, black vultures, circling in hopes of prey. Well, hell.

He went over to the window at the front of the house. In the pale gray, barely-light, he watched the column of armored vehicles pour out of the driveway and surround the house.

There in the circle, facing the front door, was a tank. At least, he thought it was a tank. Heavily armored, with a large caliber gun aimed right at the house, at point-blank range. His heart sank.

One shot from that and this whole house is ash. Shit, shit, shit... He got dressed in a hurry in the master bedroom and rushed into the dressing room. Shifting his vision, the butler wavered into view.

"Tell everyone to hide. Don't show yourselves, don't drag anyone in. Hide the bullet damage upstairs if you can, and don't let them see the icehouse."

The butler nodded and vanished as Henry ran downstairs. He'd hidden the memory crystals in the icehouse, at least that way all the incriminating evidence was all together. If they could help hide it all…

Through the windows, he saw a group setting up a battering ram for the front door. He ran to the front door and took a deep breath. Trying to maintain a calm, nonchalant affect, he opened the front door.

"Oh! Good morning. Can I help you?" he offered and closed the door behind him.

"Hands over your head. Are you alone in the house?" the helmeted figure barked.

Henry slowly raised his hands. "Sure. Yes, just me."

The figure frisked him quickly, and ordered, "Stand aside." He motioned for several others to follow him. "We are conducting a thorough search of this residence. Are there any weapons or other hazards?"

Henry stifled the shriek that rose from his belly and just smiled tightly. For the most part, outsiders rummaging through the house had never gone well, from Enrico to Valéria to McBurk to the agents… The injuries and body count was first on Henry's mind. But he had no choice.

"No, no weapons," Henry said. "But please do be careful. I've been hired to renovate the house, and we've gotten a lot of work done, but there may be… soft spots in the flooring. We've had some injuries. I just got my own cast off. I'm not sure how well the house will hold up under the weight of your armor."

The men nodded, raised their weapons, and entered the house. The door offered its usual etude of squeaks and groans. The men glanced at each other but went through the entrance hall and into the grand ballroom, dispersing through the rooms.

Well, that was not exactly unexpected.

Henry was pleased that they hadn't just blown the front door off its hinges, or that they hadn't dropped an aerial incendiary device of some sort. But he felt awkward now, just waiting on the front steps. Minutes passed slowly.

After a while, they must have deemed the house secure and Henry not a threat, as a uniformed man and a younger woman got out of one of the armored carriers. A pair of armored soldiers had been buzzing about the agents' abandoned car; they went over and talked to the two. Henry couldn't quite overhear, but he thought he heard them say, "…same as we found in McBurk's car, sir. Yes, still locked."

The two nodded, spoke quietly together, and then approached Henry.

"I'm Lieutenant Tabor, this is Officer Reynolds." The man gestured. "We'd like to ask you a few questions. May we?" He gestured to the front door.

"Of course." Henry led them in, through the entrance hall, and into the grand ballroom.

"Well, there's something you don't see every day." Tabor scanned the vast open area. He didn't like open areas.

In the war, an open area was a prime spot for an ambush. A *kill box*, they called it. He put the idea out of his mind, but asked, "Ah, is there some place we can sit and talk?"

"Of course, right this way." Henry waved them through the lobby, past a few soldiers with scanners, and into the study, and sat at the desk to face them.

"When was the last time you saw Officer Eric McBurk?" Tabor got right to it.

"McBurk?" Henry asked. "He the sort of pink-looking fellow, looks a bit like a fireplug?"

Reynolds stifled a smirk, not entirely successfully. Tabor winced. "Er, yeah, I suppose, a bit."

"Last I saw him was in the parking lot down at The Grumpy Yorkie. He was drunk off his ass and threatening folks. Me, in particular. Reggie came out and chased him off. That was, oh, day before yesterday maybe?" Henry feigned confusion.

Reynolds nodded in agreement. "Yes, we have other eyewitness reports that confirm that."

"Why was McBurk threatening you? What had you done to piss him off?" Tabor did not mince words.

"Nothing that I know of." Henry waved his hands open. "As soon as he found out I was cleaning up Weatherly and living up here, he seemed to get very… I don't know, *agitated*, I guess? He really didn't like the idea of anyone living up here. I have no idea why."

Tabor and Reynolds looked at each other. Tabor said, "I think I have an idea about that. But, before we get into that, would you mind giving us a quick tour? I've heard you've really spruced the place up."

Henry swallowed, but the soldiers were wandering freely through the house, and nothing had happened yet.

"Follow me," he said blandly.

He took them through the first floor, and they marveled at the massive kitchen, the greenhouse, billiard room, the bowling alley. They looked in all the bedrooms, took a quick pass though the main hall of the attics, and asked to see the basement.

Sure, what could go wrong?

Henry could practically feel the hairs on their necks standing at attention as they eased down the narrow staircase into the dark, dank, underground realm.

At least there are lights now. Somehow, they still didn't manage to dispel the darkness completely, but it was enough for the officers to have a good look around. They split up, looking up and down the main corridor and into the side rooms. Henry wandered aimlessly, sticking sort of to the middle in case either of them had any questions and trying not to look nervous or suspicious.

He caught a glance of the room with the drain and felt his attention shift. There, still hung up on the meat hooks, was the agent, bleeding out and whimpering. Henry whipped around to see where the two officers were, and they were both headed his way, coming in from different directions.

His brain froze. There was no way he could explain this. He started to open his mouth anyway as the officers approached, but they simply walked right past him out into the main corridor.

They can't see it.

As casually as he could, he closed his mouth and ambled back out to the main corridor. Same as with the soldiers who'd just been through, these two found nothing, and nothing found them. Tabor waved him along, and they all went back upstairs and returned to the study.

Tabor broke the silence. "Okay, here's what I think. As near as I can tell, McBurk was running some kind of drug operation."

Reynolds chimed in. "We found dodecs in his car and in his locker at the station."

Tabor nodded. "My guess is that he was using this property for something. Dead drops, probably. That's why he was so pissed you were up here all of a sudden."

It was all Henry could do to keep from bursting at the seams.

It worked. They're going to blame this all on McBurk. Holy shit!

He gurgled a genuinely surprised reply. "No kidding. Shit. Well, makes sense, I guess. This place had stood empty for a really long time."

A soldier came in and motioned to speak to Tabor. He showed him something on a tablet for a minute or two, then left.

"You didn't find anything… unusual on the property?" Tabor asked.

Henry shook his head. "Hah. This whole *house* is unusual. Old wiring that looks like jungle vines, gas lights, a kitchen oven large enough to cook an ox… but no drug factory, if that's what you're asking."

Tabor nodded. "All the scans are negative for any drug equipment, storage, anything like that, and we haven't seen any unusual traffic since you've been up here. So whatever they were doing, your presence here must have put a real crimp in it."

"Well, that makes sense, I suppose. So, he's in custody now, is that what this is about?" Henry asked, his face a picture of innocence.

"Not exactly," Reynolds replied. "McBurk disappeared after that night at the bar. We found his vehicle there the next day, but he'd turned off his sensors and tracking. There's a bulletin out for his arrest, but he hasn't turned up on any scans yet."

"Wow," Henry said. "That probably explains the two agents from Central who came by yesterday."

"You spoke to them?" Tabor asked.

"Yeah, briefly. They didn't come in past the entrance hall. Asked me how long I'd been here, if I knew McBurk. Nothing in any real detail. Then they left but not in their car. Someone came up and met them."

Henry hadn't thought this part through and was making it up as he went. He had to be careful—too much detail was a clear sign you were lying.

"Can you describe the car?" Reynolds asked, poised to take notes.

Henry thought for a moment. "Ah, I wasn't really paying close attention. It wasn't any sort of state vehicle. Just a small, plain white or light-colored model, I think. It seemed weird they left the patrol car out front. I assumed they'd come back for it. But you must have footage of all that, right?"

Henry suppressed an internal chortle at the thought. He knew he'd jammed them but good.

Tabor frowned. "Turns out, they turned off their logging and sensors as well. Which is strictly against policy. We just found some evidence that they may have been working with McBurk as well. That might have been them joining up with him here. But they're off the grid now and possibly traveling together."

"I bet they are." Henry nodded.

He really did agree that they were together now, some-where, in some version of hell or damnation. He shook his head dramatically, as if to clear it. "Wow, I mean just wow. When I took this job to oversee repairs to this es-tate, I had no idea what I was in for. I've suffered injuries, collapses, enough dust to choke an army, animals and pests invading, and now apparently I've disrupted a gang of drug dealers."

Tabor leaned back and nodded. "So it seems."

Reynolds asked him, "Will you be staying on, or are you headed back to the megapolis?"

"I'm being paid to stay on," Henry replied. "In fact, I got a message from corporate the other day with plans for a big holiday party. Everyone in town will be invited. Apparently, in the old days, this house was known for its hospitality, and I think that's what the owners are trying to recapture."

Tabor grunted. "Huh. I mean, the townsfolk would certainly appreciate it, I'm sure, but... why? What's in it for the corporation?"

Henry shook his head. "I just work here. No idea. When they first hired me, they said something about the position involving responsibilities to the community. I'm not sure what they meant by that, but they seemed serious. And they pay well. So..." Henry shrugged.

Reynolds cocked an eyebrow.

Henry nodded. "Yeah. I try to take it seriously. Hired folks from right here in town to help with the construction, electrical and plumbing and all, and some cleaning help." Henry really played the *helping your town by bringing in money* card. He hoped it helped.

Tabor stood, and Reynolds followed suit. "Thank for your time, Mr. Steward. I am bound to remind you that you are on a watch list, and I have to file a full report on the search and our interview here today. But I see no evidence of any data hoarding or processing at all, and no sign of illegal drug manufacture or other activities. You've done a good job with the house." He nodded gruffly and headed to the door.

Reynolds added in, "Looking forward to the party. Welcome to the community." She smiled.

The armored cars filed out of the front circle and down the driveway, the flock of drones tagging along behind. In moments, the property was silent again.

Out of the corner of his eye, Henry saw something white flash in the woods. He turned to look and saw a deer, white as a cloud, standing in the woods, returning his stare. They stayed like that for a few moments. The deer seemed to nod, turned, and vanished into the forest.

Henry blinked and stood still, taking in the comforting silence of the woods. He turned to the house, closed the massive front door behind him, and breathed a sigh of relief that was nearly as strong as the gust of wind through Weatherly.

Time to start planning for that party, I guess. Enrico and Paul and Pamela, Esmeralda, Fiona… they all deserve it. The whole town deserves it. Time to make Weatherly shine again.

He walked back though the cavernous grand ballroom, whistling a tune that echoed through the house. A happy tune.

He sighed loudly with relief.

Maybe it was his imagination, but he could swear the house sighed back.

Epilogue

Moonlight splashed over the ruins as the man
slowly walked up the small hill from his car. It had been
a house once, on the outskirts of town past Weatherly
Hall. There were outbuildings, or maybe it was several
small houses. Hard to tell; now it was just a collection
of crumbling walls and invasive weeds. A hooded figure
stood at the top of the hill, watching his approach, hand
in pocket.

"What do you think happened to McBurk?" the
walking man asked the hooded figure.

"Do I look like I give a shit?" she answered, keeping
the hood up and her hand on her weapon.

"You should," the man replied, his voice even. "He
was our only 'in' up here in the wilderness. Without him
making paperwork disappear, well, it makes these sorts
of transactions a whole lot more risky."

"I can take care of me and mine." She half-lifted her gun for emphasis. "I took care of a lot of those crybabies during the war. Still can. I haven't always been in 'sales.'"

He nodded, took a small cloth bag from inside his coat, and handed it to her. "Usual."

She opened the bag and shook the several wafers into her other palm, then drew a small reader from a pocket and waved it over the memory wafers. Satisfied with the enormous sums they represented, she stuffed them and the reader back inside her coat.

"In the corner of that house." She gestured toward one particular set of crumbling ruins at the edge of the no-longer buildings on the hillock.

He nodded and ducked into the building to get the latest batch of dodecs.

She started down the back of the hill toward her car when she heard the crash of ancient concrete and the screaming. Whipping the gun out of her pocket, she dove into a crouch and sprang back toward the ruins, expecting an ambush—some rival encroaching on her turf, trying to get a valuable haul of dodecs.

But there was no one there, just a cloud of dust rising from a wall that had caved in. Remains of the man's legs oozed out from under the crumbled concrete and rock. She wondered for a moment if she might be able to dig through the rubble and reclaim the dodecs herself.

But she didn't have to wonder long, as the floor suddenly dissolved underneath her. She fired a wild shot in the air but then lost the gun as she smashed her head and upper torso against the hard concrete floor.

Blood poured into her eyes. She wiped at her face furiously but couldn't see straight. It looked like the floor was at about elbow height, and the rest of her body was gone. She blinked more blood out of her eyes.

Screaming, she realized that her lower body was, indeed, gone. In or under the floor, it didn't matter, it was no longer attached. She flopped about, screaming, briefly.

Past the bottom of the hill, at the edge of the woods, Henry smiled. He walked out into the moonlight and pulled a sheet of paper from his pocket. Carefully, he crossed her name off the list and began walking back through to the other side of the woods where he had parked.

It was a clear night and cold. Henry walked alone though the normally dark woods, brilliant now in the moonlight.

Not really alone, though, am I? Henry grinned and saw a glimpse of shadows moving through the trees.

Such a beautiful night.

Thank You!

Thank you for reading *Weatherly Hall*, I hope you enjoyed it. Please help others find this book:

1. Lend a copy to a friend
2. Write a review on Amazon, Goodreads, blogs
3. Sign up for the new releases/goodies e-mail on my website at conglommora.com

Enjoy!

About the Author

Andy Hunt is an author, publisher, consultant, and programmer. He has authored award-winning and best-selling books, including the seminal classic *The Pragmatic Programmer*, *Learn to Program with Minecraft Plugins* for the kids, the perennially popular *Pragmatic Thinking and Learning: Refactor Your Wetware*, the Jolt-award winning *Practices of An Agile Developer*, and more. When not writing, Andy is an active musician and woodworker. Visit Andy's home page at www.toolshed.com to see what he's up to now.

Conglommora

The Green Earth of old was long gone. The People printed their ships and fled the devastation to find another planet, a new home. But system after system, planet after planet, they discovered there were no other suitable homes in the cosmos. So they joined their ships together here at the edge of Nothing to form the Conglommora: a massive, stationary, ad-hoc, self-sufficient world hundreds of light-years out in deep space. Until a mysterious straggler from Dead Earth plummets them into a startling journey across the galaxy, to confront the past and threaten the future. Available at Amazon.com and conglommora.com.

Conglommora Found

Charlie Neylan and his son Alain thought their adventures were over, as they settled into the shape of their new lives on Conglommora. But things get complicated as Alain risks his life to find answers to the secrets of their world, and their very world gets a lot larger than anyone thought. The new hidden undersea base, Denisova, expanded their world. So much new to study, so much to see—but safely, hidden from their descendants. The good People of Conglommora couldn't reveal themselves without jeopardizing their future. They had to keep them isolated, alone. What was left of humanity was utterly alone. Until it wasn't. Available at Amazon.com and conglommora.com.

The Pragmatic Programmer: 20th Anniversay Edition

The most-recommended book on software development, and an Amazon top-ten best seller. This new 20th Anniversary Edition offers a fresh look at the modern development landscape, cutting through the "business as usual" and tired advice from the net to help guide you through the next twenty years and beyond.

Featuring new tips, new topics, and revisions throughout, you don't want to miss this one. Available at Amazon.com and pragprog.com.

Practices of an Agile Developer

My friend Venkat had this great idea for a book: the personal practices, habits, and approaches that really work and will make you a better developer. You'll learn pragmatic ways of approaching the development process and your personal coding techniques. You'll learn about your own attitudes, issues with working on a team, and how to best manage your learning, all in an iterative, incremental, agile style. You'll see how to apply each practice, and what benefits you can expect. Bottom line: This book will make you a better developer. Available at Amazon.com and pragprog.com.

Pragmatic Thinking & Learning: Refactor Your Wetware

Improve your thinking and learning skills, boost your creativity, and invest in your most important asset: your mind. Programmers have to learn constantly; not just the stereotypical new technologies, but also the problem domain of the application, the whims of the user community, the quirks of your teammates, the shifting sands of the industry, and the evolving characteristics of the project itself as it is built. We'll journey together through bits of cognitive and neuroscience, learning and behavioral theory. You'll see some surprising aspects of how our brains work, and how you can take advantage of the system to improve your own learning and thinking skills. Available at Amazon.com and pragprog.com.

www.ingramcontent.com/pod-product-compliance
Lightning Source LLC
Chambersburg PA
CBHW031941110726
47902CB00001B/262